"Open your e[yes...]

Tom stilled the m[ovement...] let me touch the fire deep inside you," he murmured, kissing Cleo's jaw, her cheeks. "Let me see the fire in your eyes when I take you over the edge."

Slowly her eyes opened, pale yet glowing in the dim light of the clearing.

His breath caught in his throat. He increased the pressure, quickened the rhythm and watched with a fierce sense of possession as the flame leapt into her eyes. "Yes," he whispered as he felt her excitement. Whether she knew it or not, he was staking a claim tonight.

Her eyes darkened. With a soft cry of surrender, she lifted her hips, allowing him even deeper penetration as she shook with the force of her climax. When she relaxed in his arms a few minutes later, he slowly withdrew his hand, gave her one last lingering kiss and climbed out of the hot tub.

"Tom?" Her voice was husky with spent passion. "You're...leaving. But..."

He gazed at her silently, his mind warring against the grinding need to take her. Then he turned. "A smart cowboy lets a filly get used to him before he tries to ride her for the first time."

Dear Reader,

When I first heard about Temptation's newest miniseries, I was thrilled. After all, here was a theme I could really sink my teeth into. You see, I've actually been on a "manhunt." Once, when I was single, my sister decided I needed to find a guy. Since I've always had a weakness for cowboys, we went "manhunting" at a country-western dance hall. The room was awash in snug jeans, shiny belt buckles, leather boots and Stetsons. Yet somehow I ended up giving my phone number to the only guy in the place dressed in slacks and a sports shirt. Go figure.

My instincts must have been right, because we've been married twenty-eight years. But in that time, a gradual transformation has taken place. First came the jeans. Then the boots. Finally, not long ago, he bought a Western hat in a secondhand shop, a broken-in model that's already loaded with character. Looks like I found me a cowboy after all.

Happy reading,

Vicki Lewis Thompson

Vicki Lewis Thompson

Manhunting
in Montana

Harlequin Books

TORONTO • NEW YORK • LONDON
AMSTERDAM • PARIS • SYDNEY • HAMBURG
STOCKHOLM • ATHENS • TOKYO • MILAN
MADRID • WARSAW • BUDAPEST • AUCKLAND

For Kathleen Stone, whose unbridled enthusiasm has
earned her another cowboy.
Enjoy, Kathy!
And special thanks to Aline and Jim Moore,
my Montana buddies.

ISBN 0-373-25777-5

MANHUNTING IN MONTANA

Copyright © 1998 by Vicki Lewis Thompson.

Printed in U.S.A.

SHOOTING GORGEOUS GUYS really turned her on.

Cleo Griffin returned to her New York studio in the condition that usually followed a photo session—she wanted to grab the nearest man and get naked. Unfortunately there was no man in her studio, only her assistant and best friend, Bernadette Fairchild.

Bernie, a Rosie O'Donnell look-alike, glanced up from the computer screen. "You're flushed."

"Of course I'm flushed." Cleo took a bite of the soft pretzel she'd bought from a street vendor. Then, laying the pretzel on Bernie's desk, she eased the heavy camera bag off her shoulder onto an office chair.

"I take it Mr. December was well put-together?"

Cleo headed for the watercooler. "Bernie, the pecs on that guy would make you weep." She filled a paper cup with water and gulped it down. "If I don't get some action soon, I'm gonna self-combust."

Bernie stopped typing and swiveled her chair toward Cleo. "There's this new thing I just heard of. Dating."

"Don't have time." Cleo crumpled the paper cup and threw it in the trash before glancing at Bernie. "You're lucky. You have George to go home to."

"I invested *two years* in Project George. That's not luck, that's top-level strategy."

"I should have done the same thing when I was in school."

"Didn't I tell you that? Didn't I tell you those were the mating years? But would you listen?"

"It's not too late." Cleo pulled a chair over in front of Bernie's desk and sat down. "I can still find somebody. All I need is a nice guy who won't interfere with my work."

"But someone talented enough to take the edge off after a steamy session behind the lens, right?"

Cleo crossed her ankle over her knee and grinned. "That goes without saying." She picked up her pretzel again and took a generous bite.

"I'm afraid they don't offer those in the *Sharper Image* catalog," Bernie said. "By the way, your tickets arrived for the Montana trip. You're staying at a small, intimate yet authentic guest ranch, just like you specified. Six cabins, so it won't be crawling with tourists, and Tom McBride, the owner, runs a few head of cattle, so you'll have plenty of cowboys on the property and more at neighboring ranches." She pushed an envelope across the desk.

"Cowboys." Cleo picked up the envelope to look inside and check flight times. "How am I ever going to survive shooting twelve hunky cowhands, considering the shape I'm in after finishing this firefighter calendar?"

Bernie resumed typing. "Give in and take one to bed."

"No." She'd been tempted so many times, but it was totally unprofessional. She had a reputation to protect.

"You'll be at the ends of the earth in Montana." Bernie clicked the mouse on the print command and sat back in her chair. "I think they still communicate by

Pony Express out there. Word would never get back to New York that you'd been naughty."

Cleo finished off the pretzel. "You know me better than that. I couldn't live with myself. Besides, it's almost as if I have to keep doing everything the same, with no deviation, to keep this calendar bonanza going."

"Chick, you're there. You've made it." Bernie picked up the letter that rolled out of the laser printer. "Are your hands clean?"

Cleo licked pretzel salt from her thumb. "Not exactly."

"Then don't touch this." She laid it in front of Cleo. "I just want you to read it and gloat."

Cleo read the letter explaining to the Van Cleefs that Ms. Griffin's schedule wouldn't allow her to photograph their daughter's very expensive, very prestigious wedding. Five years ago when the oldest daughter had gotten married, Bernie had practically crawled over broken glass trying to get Cleo the job, but another photographer had been chosen. Cleo knew she should be as impressed as Bernie that they didn't need the Van Cleefs anymore. She wanted to feel secure and confident with her success, but most of the time she felt more like a tightrope walker balancing a tray of Fabergé eggs.

She glanced up. "Okay, so I'm not begging to take society-wedding shots these days, but—"

"Your *Hard-Hat Heroes* calendar almost outsold *Calvin and Hobbes* last Christmas."

"Almost isn't good enough."

Bernie let out an exasperated sigh. "And would that be another maxim from the great Calvin Griffin?"

"Well, he's right." Cleo wadded up the paper the

pretzel had come in and got out of the chair to throw it away. Talking about her father always made her edgy. "He didn't *almost* become the CEO of Sphinx Cosmetics. He's never *almost* done anything." Except once, she thought. He'd *almost* fathered a son, until Cleo's mother had miscarried, leaving him with only a daughter.

"Aren't you the CEO of Griffin Studios?" Bernie said quietly.

"It's not the same. It's not—"

"Enough?" Bernie prompted. "Listen, kid, you shouldn't have to prove anything to—"

"I need to get this film labeled and ready for the lab." Cleo picked up the camera bag by the strap. "The contact sheets won't be finished before I leave for Montana tomorrow, so you'll have to overnight them to me at the guest ranch. What's the name of it?"

"The Whispering Winds."

"Sounds way too romantic to be authentic. A ranch is supposed to be named something like the Triple Bar or the Rocking Z."

"I suggest you tell Tom McBride that. I'm sure he'd appreciate the tip from a New Yorker." Bernie returned to her keyboard.

"Well, I just might. The right name could improve his business." Cleo started toward her workroom. The studio was small—nine hundred square feet that included a reception area, Cleo's workroom and a seldom-used cubicle set up with umbrella lights for studio shots. Ever since Cleo had hit upon the idea of creating hunk calendars, she'd pretty much abandoned studio photography. She preferred shooting her men in their natural environment.

"Why not choose thirteen this time?" Bernie called after her.

Cleo turned back. "Thirteen what?"

"Cowboys. Pick out an extra one. Then if there's one of the thirteen you like personally, and he likes you, eliminate him from the calendar and make a little whoopee. You'll have some fun and you won't compromise your professional ethics."

Cleo rested the camera bag on the floor as she gazed at Bernie. The idea that was slowly forming terrified her, but it could be the answer to her prayers. "You just might have something there."

"That's my job. Facilitating your career and your happiness. You can have a wonderful romp in Montana and come home with a calendar and some great memories."

"I could also come home with a husband." God, that sounded bizarre. But what if her raging hormones caused her to forget herself during a shoot one of these days? She could ruin her reputation, her self-respect and her career in one fell swoop.

Bernie stared at her. "Hey, wait a minute, Cleo. That's not what I—"

"Why not?" Cleo met the fear churning inside with her usual weapon—an outward show of supreme confidence. "My interview for the bio note on the calendar can do double duty as a potential-husband questionnaire. I can kill two birds with one stone. It's perfect."

"Love doesn't work on that kind of efficiency model, toots."

Cleo lifted her chin. "I say it can." Even Bernie didn't know how desperate she'd become for safe, steady sexual release with an understanding man, or how lonely her downtime had become when she was between projects. Marriage was the only solution. But she had to find some way to work the selection process into her schedule. Crazy as it seemed, this could be the answer.

Bernie didn't seem to appreciate the beauty of her plan. "Even if you managed such a thing, then what?" she argued. "You'll drag some poor cowboy back to New York? According to the movies, those ol' boys like the wide-open spaces, the howl of Wily Coyote, the smell of horse poop. You can't expect him to survive on the aroma of cab fumes."

"No, I wouldn't drag him back to New York. That's why it would be so perfect. He could stay in Montana, and I'd stay in New York, and we'd get together on weekends whenever it was convenient. I could go there, he could come here or we could each fly to a central spot like, say, Chicago."

Bernie stared at her with her mouth hanging open. "You're really serious."

"Of course." She was quivering inside, but she was deadly serious.

"What happens when the little bambinos show up? Will they be centrally located in Kansas?"

"No bambinos," she said quickly, thinking of how children could wreck her career. "That will be understood from the beginning. Not every guy wants to have kids, you know. Don't worry. I'll find one who thinks a commuter marriage is an exciting way to live."

"Cleo, are you nuts? This is too outrageous, my little bohemian friend, even for you."

"It is exactly what I need, and it is exactly what I'm going to get. Thanks for the idea, Bernie."

"That was *not* my idea. Don't you dare go pinning the

rap on me. All I suggested was some R and R, not a husband-hunting expedition."

"But don't you see? I don't have time for R and R, but I have to solve this problem, and soon."

"What's wrong with you? Marriage is about sharing your life with someone! All you'd share would be sex and an accumulation of frequent-flier miles!"

"I'm going to do it, Bernie. I'm not saying it'll be easy finding a husband in two weeks, but you know how much I love challenges." Cleo swallowed the nervous lump in her throat. This had to work. "Somewhere in Montana, right this minute, my future husband is roping a steer, or sipping coffee beside a campfire, or riding a bucking bronco—one of those manly things cowboys do—unaware that his life is about to change forever."

"Or at least on alternate weekends," Bernie said.

"TOM, the toilet don't work in cabin six, and that photographer from New York is due in there tomorrow."

Tom McBride looked away from the computer terminal on his desk, more than happy to be interrupted. No matter how he juggled the figures, the Whispering Winds was sinking deeper in debt every year. He glanced up at the slim cowboy, Jeeter Neff, who stood just inside the open door of his office. Tom treated the men and women working for him on the ranch as equals, and the only people on the place who called him Mr. McBride were his cook Juanita's two kids, at Juanita's insistence.

"Is Hank around somewhere?" Tom asked. Hank Jacobs was the ranch's official handyman, a weathered old guy who'd been a school janitor before finally getting his wish to work and live as a cowboy.

"You gave him a week off to get his mother settled in that old folks' home."

"Oh yeah."

"I'd see to it, but I'm s'posed to take the Daniels bunch out on a trail ride in about ten minutes, and from what Luann said when she was in there gettin' the place ready, something needs to be done pronto."

Tom pushed back his chair, glad for an excuse to leave the office and the sea of red on the computer screen. He stood and grabbed his hat from the peg on the wall. "I'll do it."

"I'd recommend taking a plunger," Jeeter said with a grin. "Maybe a snake, too."

"On second thought, maybe I should wrangle the Daniels bunch and you can deal with the toilet."

Jeeter backed up, poised to hightail it out the front door of the ranch house. "You know, I never was much good at that job. Usually ended up making a worse mess than when I got started."

"Handy excuse, Jeeter." Another thought occurred to Tom. He hadn't considered the ramifications of giving Hank the time off. "I guess that means Hank can't pick up that photographer at the airport tomorrow, either."

"I guess not."

Tom sighed. "I might as well do it, then. Somebody needs to take a manure sample to the lab for a worm check, anyhow. Might as well get 'em both done at once."

"You gonna take that sample in before or after you go to the airport?"

"I don't know. Depends on traffic. Why?"

Jeeter's grin broke through again. "I just don't know if it'll do much for business, hauling around some fancy-dancy woman from New York with a plastic bag full of road apples on the seat between you."

"Hey, I talked to her secretary. This lady wants an *authentic* ranching experience." Tom didn't believe that for a minute. They all said that, until you handed them a shovel or asked them to stretch some barbed wire. "You just made up my mind, Jeeter. I'm taking in the sample after I pick her up. Let's see what she's made of."

Jeeter laughed and took off.

Moments later, armed with a plunger, Tom stepped out onto the wide front porch of the ranch house. He'd been born in this house, had learned to walk on this porch while clutching the railing. An errand had to be pretty damned important to keep him from pausing to appreciate the view from the top of the steps, and the toilet wasn't that important.

Although his dad had never been much for "standin' and gawkin'," his mother had taught him to treasure what lay before him—a meadow greening up after a rain, a corral of sleek horses, outbuildings nestled into the trees, and beyond, the proud sweep of the Gallatins still tipped with snow on this June morning. He knew the imprint of those mountains against the sky as well as he knew his mother's face. *Not many folks have paradise right out their front door, Tommy*, she'd said more times than he could count.

He took a deep breath of the pine-scented air. Friends had advised him to build more guest cabins to bring in the money he needed to stay solvent, but that would change the character of the ranch he loved more than anyone knew. Tugging at the brim of his Stetson, he left the porch and started toward cabin six. He wasn't good at compromise. And it might eventually get him kicked right out of paradise.

TOM HADN'T BEEN on airport duty for some time, and he arrived at the terminal with nothing more than the flight's arrival to go by. He'd forgotten to find the photographer's name in the computer before he left the Whispering Winds, but there couldn't be that many women on the plane with a big-city air and a camera bag over one shoulder.

Come to think of it, he hadn't been to the airport since the last time he'd met Deidre there two years ago. No wonder he was in a rotten mood, with memories of his ex-wife floating around the place. Deidre had looked fantastic coming down the jetway, he remembered, but professional models were supposed to look fantastic. Apparently they weren't supposed to look pregnant.

He'd waited for her, the medical report in his hand, hoping there had been some mistake. No mistake. She'd had the abortion in New York and never meant for him to know. The clinic had screwed up by accidentally sending the bill to her Montana address. Once Tom understood completely what had happened, it hadn't been Deidre's address any longer.

And here he was waiting for another woman who worked in New York. Unfair as it might be, he'd already branded the two as coming from the same herd. Although Deidre made her living in front of the camera and this woman made hers behind it, both of them had chosen a world in which image was everything.

Truth be told, he didn't much relish the idea of transporting this citified woman who wanted to photograph "authentic" cowboys. Jeeter would tell him he had a sizable chip on his shoulder about it, and Jeeter would be right. Tom had driven the truck through several mud puddles before he hit the main highway leading to the Bozeman airport, and the plastic bag of manure rested right on the dash, where the morning sun could bring out its special aroma. He'd worn his most faded blue work shirt, his most battered hat and the jeans that he'd torn up on the barbed wire the last time he'd been fixing fence.

As the plane carrying his New York guest landed, Tom remembered there was a little trick for notifying off-loading folks that you were their ride home. He ought to be holding a sign, and because he didn't remember the woman's name he'd have to write Whispering Winds on it. He glanced around for something to write on, but there was precious little presenting itself.

Finally he noticed a newspaper in the trash. It turned out to be a scandal sheet, and the biggest expanse of light-colored space to write on was that occupied by Loni Anderson's cleavage in a white sequined dress. Tom borrowed a pen from a businessman working a crossword puzzle and lettered a bold Whispering Winds across Loni's chest. Then in parentheses he added Run by Authentic Cowboys. Returning the pen, he folded the newspaper so the writing was facing toward the people getting off the plane.

There she was. He'd bet money that was her—a sleek brunette covered with gold jewelry and carrying nothing but one of those dumb little purses that looked as if it would barely hold a credit card and some loose change. Maybe she'd checked her camera equipment along with her luggage. Her outfit, tight jeans and a leather vest with lots of fringe, was exactly what New Yorkers might think they should wear in Montana.

He held up his tabloid sign and gazed at the brunette. She walked right past him, trailing clouds of heavy perfume. He was so surprised, so certain he'd been right, that he called after her, "Whispering Winds, ma'am!"

"I believe you're looking for me," said a low voice right beside him.

He turned and looked into her eyes. *Montana-sky blue.* The ranch hands would laugh themselves silly if they knew he'd thought such a thing, but it was true. He didn't have to look down very far to see into her eyes, either. She stood at least five-nine or ten, with curly golden hair falling in a jumble past her shoulders. It looked in need of a combing, and Tom had the crazy urge to straighten it out a little by running his fingers through it.

Over a blue work shirt almost as faded as his, she wore a canvas vest with all sorts of pockets, and her slacks were on the baggy side, not designed to show off what he suspected was a decent figure. She carried a heavy-looking camera bag over one shoulder, a backpack over the other, and held a wheeled carry-on by the handle. She was rumpled, appealing, and smelled as if she'd been rolling in wildflowers. She was nothing like what he'd expected.

He remembered the manure on the dash and winced.

"Cleo Griffin." Her clipped accent gave her away as a New Yorker and brought back memories of Deidre. She hoisted the camera bag more firmly on her shoulder and held out her hand.

He snapped out of his fog and realized that he'd been letting a ranch guest stand there laden down like a pack animal. "Let me take that, ma'am," he said, reaching for the camera-bag strap instead of accepting her handshake.

"I'll keep it, thanks." She made a quick grab for the strap and grabbed his hand instead.

Her grip was warm and firm, her skin smooth against his. As his gaze locked with hers for just an instant, he felt an unexpected rush of pleasure. All his memories of Deidre weren't bad, and this woman triggered the good ones, too.

She released his hand and took hold of the strap. "I need to be in charge of my equipment." Her tone was all business, but there was something going on in those blue eyes of hers that looked like more than business. She unhooked the backpack from her other shoulder. "I'd appreciate it if you'd take this, though. It's full of books, and it's getting very heavy."

He swung the backpack to his shoulder. "Is there more?"

She looked startled. "More what?"

"Luggage."

"Than this?" She gestured toward her rolling suitcase and the backpack. "I should hope not. I'm not planning on attending any fancy-dress balls or—" She paused. "Oh, I get it. I'm a woman, so of course I've arrived with fourteen suitcases."

"Now, ma'am, I didn't mean—"

"Yes, you did, but never mind." She tapped the newspaper he still held in one hand. "Tell me, is this part of the dude treatment?"

He'd forgotten all about the sign he'd printed across Loni Anderson's cleavage. "I wanted to get your attention."

"Well, Loni's chest as an attention-getter is a little off the mark. Next time you're meeting a woman at the airport, try Matt McConaughey's chest and see if that doesn't work better."

He held back a grin. "Yes, ma'am."

She looked him up and down, her gaze amused. "From all these ma'ams you're tossing around, I gather you're one of the authentic cowboys who runs the Whispering Winds."

She had a smart mouth on her, but he was kind of enjoying the exchange. She might be more fun to have around than he'd thought. "Montana born and bred."

"Good. That's exactly what I'm looking for. Shall we leave?"

Tom touched the brim of his hat. "At your service, ma'am." This time when he thought about the manure on the dash, he smiled.

2

GOD, he was magnificent, Cleo thought, lengthening her stride to keep up with the lean cowboy beside her. She had to have him, chauvinism and all. Montana born and bred, indeed, unflappable as the rugged Rockies. His self-confidence would come across when she photographed him, making him a perfect cover model for the calendar.

Choosing him for the cover would eliminate him from the husband hunt, but he wouldn't have made the cut, anyway. He wasn't tame enough, which made him perfect cover material. The idea of capturing this man on film commanded her complete attention.

She'd begin with a full-length shot, maybe pose him leaning against a weathered fence with a coiled rope in one hand. She wanted to reach beneath the veneer of nonchalance he presented to the world and hint at the intensity simmering below the surface. The lens would love those broad shoulders and slim hips. Then she'd move in for some close-ups to bring out the flinty cast of his eyes and capture that mocking look he'd given her when she'd asked if he was an authentic cowboy.

As they crossed the parking lot in bright sunshine, she glanced over to see how the light affected the contours of his face. His battered hat shadowed most of it, but the sun found its way to the squared-off angle of his chin. Just below his lower lip a scar formed a white crescent against his tan. Beneath his hat, the hair at his temples and his nape was warm brown streaked with sun. The creases in his cheeks and the crinkle lines at the corners of his eyes revealed that he found life amusing a good deal of the time.

"Checking to see if I washed behind my ears this morning?" he asked without turning his head.

"No, I'm thinking of exactly how I'd like to photograph you."

He stopped abruptly and swung to face her. "No way, Ms. Griffin."

She backed up a step, amazed at the sudden hostility in his expression. "Let me put it this way. I pay really well, and it could easily be the best thing that ever happened to you. Men who've been in my calendars have been swamped with all sorts of offers, from movie contracts to marriage."

That mocking look reappeared in his gray eyes. "I have no desire to be in the movies, or to get married again. As for the money, you couldn't pay me enough to gallivant around in front of a camera and hang on the wall like some centerfold."

"My subject's don't *gallivant*, and they're not centerfolds, either. I shoot in black and white, and although the calendars are extremely commercial, I consider them art, a celebration of the beauty of the male body at work." Startled by her own outburst, she realized she'd never said those words out loud, and she was embarrassed to have spilled her creative guts in front of this cowboy. God knows why she had.

His tone gentled, and so did the look in his eyes. "Look, there are lots of men around here who will be overjoyed to pose for you. I'm just not in the market."

With every nuance of expression on his face, she became more sure that he could be one of the best subjects she'd ever photographed. Toughness and compassion didn't often go together, and her instincts told her that if she could portray that, she'd have done something worth the admiration of anyone...including her father.

She cleared her throat and tried again. "I don't think you understand. My calendars sell astronomically. The one I'm shooting now, *Montana Men*, promises to be the biggest seller of them all. I want to put you on the cover. It would literally change your life."

"Thank you, but I like my life just fine the way it is. Now I think we need to get going." He turned and started down a line of parked cars. "I have an errand to run before we head back to the ranch, and a pile of paperwork to do this afternoon."

The statement didn't sound like the kind usually made by a ranch hand. Cleo caught up with him, her suitcase wheels rattling over the asphalt. "You never did tell me your name."

"McBride. Tom McBride."

The owner of the Whispering Winds. That would explain the character she'd seen etched in his face and his uncommon poise. Putting him on the cover of the calendar would be more of a coup than she'd thought. The bio would practically compose itself and be the linchpin of her work. Tom McBride didn't know it yet, but she *would* have him for the cover.

What she needed was more information so she could plan her campaign. "I'm surprised that the owner of Whispering Winds is providing airport shuttle service," she said.

"The guy who usually does it is away on personal

business, and I had an errand in Bozeman, anyway. We'll be taking a little detour back toward town before we start down to the ranch."

"That's fine." She was a little reluctant to leave civilization, anyway. On the plane ride out here, she'd realized how much she depended on the amenities of the city to sustain her erratic eating and sleeping habits. She'd probably be expected to get up at cockcrow if she wanted breakfast at the Whispering Winds, and she doubted there was a corner deli within walking distance if she happened to oversleep.

Considering that Tom wasn't used to picking up guests at the airport, his story about finding the tabloid at the last minute so that he could make a sign to signal to her might be absolutely true. Maybe scrawling the message across Loni Anderson's chest hadn't been a chauvinistic gesture, after all. But she shouldn't forget that he'd added the words *Run by Authentic Cowboys*, which was a deliberate dig. And one he'd expected to get away with. He was one cool customer.

She watched as he approached the passenger side of a pickup truck so spattered with mud she wasn't sure what color it was. A person would have to deliberately hit puddles to get a truck that dirty, she thought.

After surveying the truck, his raggedy jeans and well-used cowboy hat, she came to a conclusion. "You know what I think, Tom?"

He paused in the act of opening the door of the unlocked truck and glanced at her. "I haven't the foggiest."

"I think you've got a wee bit of attitude."

His mouth twitched, and eventually a grin appeared. "Is that a fact?"

She approached the truck and turned over the handle of her suitcase to him so he could put it in the back. In the process, she looked directly into his eyes and smiled. "The thing is, I'm a New York chick. I was weaned on attitude, and I refuse to take B.S. from anybody. I..." She paused and wrinkled her nose at an unpleasant smell coming from the cab. "What *is* that?"

Tom seemed to be working hard not to laugh. "That would be B.S., ma'am."

She looked inside and noticed a plastic bag on the dashboard that held a substance she vaguely recognized as appearing on the pavement after parades. The smell filled the cab, but it might all be coming from that bag, which was sitting in the sun.

She faced him again. "Is this your idea of cowboy humor?"

"No, ma'am." His voice was thick with repressed laughter. "It's my idea of a lab test to see if my cows have worms. That's my errand."

She stared at him dispassionately. "I don't believe you for a minute. You planted that there to see how I'd react."

"I'll prove my story by driving straight to the lab and taking the bag of manure inside."

"That won't prove a damn thing. Why is it in the cab instead of in the back?"

"Doesn't bother me to have it in the cab."

"I see." So it was a test, she thought. "If I ride all the way to the lab with this thing smelling up the atmosphere, will you let me take your picture for my calendar?"

"Nope."

"Then I see no need to make the sacrifice." She

stepped around him, reached into the cab and took the bag by two fingers. Then she marched to the back and dropped the bag into the truck bed. Finally she climbed into the passenger seat. "I'll take my backpack and suitcase up here with me."

"You'll be mighty crowded."

"I'd rather be crowded than have my belongings shift around on that slippery truck bed and possibly smash into your bag of B.S."

"I'd hate that, too."

"Oh, sure you would."

"I would. I need that sample for the lab." He lifted her suitcase into the cab.

As she wedged it between her knees, she breathed in the woodsy scent of his aftershave, which was a welcome relief from *eau de manure*. "I'm surprised you didn't slap a little of the contents of that bag on yourself, for added effect."

He handed her the backpack. "That might have been taking things a little far."

"So you have limits to how much you tease the greenhorns?" She balanced the backpack on her suitcase and held her camera bag on her lap.

"To be honest, we don't usually tease them unless they specifically ask to meet some authentic cowboys." He closed the door and walked around to the driver's side.

"But my assistant had to ask!" she said once he got in. "Otherwise I might have ended up at some touristy place with a lot of rhinestone cowboys hanging around. I wanted the real thing."

Tom started the truck. "Well, I reckon that's what

you'll get at the Whispering Winds, ma'am," he said, his voice an exaggerated drawl.

Not if I don't get you, she thought. And Cleo always got her man.

THEY WERE PACKED so tight into the cab that Tom kept brushing Cleo's knee when he shifted gears. She seemed totally unconcerned about it, but he found the constant contact unnerving because, fight it though he tried, he was attracted to her.

In fact, the evidence was mounting that he had a thing for city gals, possibly because they were different and brought variety to his country life. He remembered taking Deidre camping once, and making love to her under the stars. Just knowing the level of her sophistication, and that he'd stripped it all away along with her clothes, was a turn-on.

At Cleo's request he stopped for some fast-food hamburgers after he dropped the manure sample at the lab. From the way she tucked into hers as they started out of town, he figured she hadn't had much to eat on the plane ride.

He was a regular fool for beauty in a woman, and he couldn't help the enjoyment he felt watching Cleo do such a simple thing as unwrap her hamburger and take a bite of it with those even white teeth of hers. Her mouth was full and wide, a generous mouth, the kind that tempted a man to nibble and taste.

She took a napkin from the sack and wiped a dab of catsup from the corner of her mouth. "I need to ask about kitchen privileges," she said.

"Kitchen privileges? You fixing to cook while you're there?"

"Not cook, exactly, but I like to eat at odd times. I guess you could say I'm a snacker. I was wondering if I'd be allowed in the kitchen to fix myself something to eat."

Tom thought about Juanita's reign in the ranch kitchen. "I doubt it, but if you're real good to our cook, she might feed you between meals."

"I'd rather take care of myself, thanks. If you'll pull into that convenience store, I'll pick up some candy bars."

Tom swung the truck into the parking lot of the store and she began to untangle herself from her luggage.

"Hey, I'll get what you need," he said as he unbuckled his seat belt. "Don't go disturbing the balance there. Just tell me what you like."

"Okay." For the first time, she presented him with a genuine smile. "Anything with chocolate and nuts."

The result of that open smile was pretty impressive.

He totally forgot what she'd just told him about her candy-bar preferences. "Sorry, you'll have to repeat that."

"Chocolate and nuts." She gazed at him. "How did you get that scar on your chin?"

He touched the scar out of habit. "A little filly kicked me years back. She didn't mean to. Just scared."

"Tom, what would it take to convince you to be photographed?"

The effect of her smile wore off. "More than you can possibly imagine." He opened the door and got out of the truck. "How many candy bars?"

"At least thirty."

He ducked his head down to stare at her. "Thirty?"

"Yes." She dug in a pocket of her vest. "Let me get you some mon—"

"I'll cover it. I just never figured you wanted thirty candy bars."

"I told you. I like to snack."

"Slight understatement." Tom went inside and cleaned out the candy counter. He had to admit it was a refreshing change from most women he knew, who'd scarcely admit they ate candy, let alone send a man they barely knew into a store to buy them thirty bars of it.

When he returned with the plastic bag and gave it to her, she thanked him and immediately delved into the assortment.

"You don't have some sort of condition, do you?" he asked.

She laughed. "Yes. It's called a high metabolism. I don't sleep much, but I sure do need to eat a lot to keep my energy level up. My dad's like that, too. I guess I inherited it."

As she unwrapped the candy, he pulled back into traffic. He was already tired of driving in it and longed for the lonely roads in the mountains. "I'd say it comes from living in New York City."

"You would, would you? Have you ever been there?"

"Yep."

"What for?"

"My ex-wife had an apartment there. Come to think of it, she probably still does."

"Now that's a fascinating bit of information." She took a bite of the candy bar.

He could tell she didn't want to drop the subject entirely, and sure enough, she brought it up again.

"I realize this is personal, and you don't have to answer, but would you consider telling me what your wife does in New York? It's a smaller town than you might think. I might even know her."

"Oh, I reckon you do. She's Deidre Anton."

Cleo sat up straighter. "The model?"

"Yep." He could almost hear the conclusions forming in her mind.

"And that's why you won't pose for me, isn't it?" she asked.

"That's the bulk of it. I've got nothing against you personally, but that whole world of glamour makes me sick to my stomach. Reality has been airbrushed right out of those pictures, but people think they're real, and then they try to be like those airbrushed folks, which they can't be, of course, so they're frustrated and unhappy with themselves."

"But I don't airbrush the men in my calendars. I like the character lines in their faces. If I photographed you, I'd want that little scar to stay in, because it's part of who you are. I'd want—"

"Cleo, I'm not doing it, so you can talk all day if you want, but it won't make any difference. I said Deidre was the main reason, but the other part is that I'm a very private man. I wouldn't want my picture all over the place."

She sighed and readjusted her knees around the suitcase. "That's a real shame."

"I can't see what the big problem is. I might be the first cowboy you've seen out here, but I won't be the last. Jeeter's going to love the idea of posing for you, I'll bet. And Stan's a pretty good-looking guy, and you might want to consider Jose, if he'll do it, which he probably will, especially if you give him that pitch about the movies. Is that part for real?"

"It's for real. I know of three guys I've used in calendars who've had small parts in movies. One just got his first speaking role."

Tom shuddered. "I'd rather be staked naked to an anthill."

"What a cool idea for a shot!"

"Not to a Montana man, it isn't. We're not that many generations removed from the pioneers who sometimes ended up that way. Anyway, you shouldn't have any trouble coming up with cowboys. There are lots of ranches around here. If this is a calendar, you only need twelve, right?"

"Well, I'd like to shoot an extra this time, in case someone doesn't work out. I don't want to have to come back."

"Yeah, that would be terrible." Tom cast her a sideways glance and was gratified that she had the sensitivity to blush, at least.

"I didn't mean it the way it sounded," she said.

"You have some beautiful country here." As if to prove that she meant it, she glanced out the window. "Really beautiful," she said with more conviction this time.

He remained silent and let the view of the mountains work on her some. Each section of Montana had something special about it, but Tom had a fierce love for Gallatin Canyon. A two-lane highway, partnered by the Gallatin River, wound between the Madison and Gallatin ranges and eventually entered Yellowstone Park. Between Bozeman and Yellowstone a person could see some damn fine scenery, in Tom's opinion.

This part of the state had been treated to some good rain the first couple of weeks of June, decorating the meadows with red Indian paintbrush, purple lupine, yellow bells and bluebells. Tom had always thought that the wildflowers, being temporary and delicate, gave a nice balance to the solid permanence of the mountains. The river flashed in the sun, reminding him of the hours he'd spent fly-fishing in its icy waters.

Cleo mumbled something as she continued to gaze out the window.

"I didn't catch that," Tom said.

"Should have brought a large-format," she said.

"Absolutely. I'm never without one, myself. What the hell is a large-format?"

She continued to be mesmerized by the view outside the truck. "It uses larger film and requires a tripod, so you can't be as spontaneous with it. I stick with the thirty-five millimeter for my calendar work, but for landscapes like this, a large format would be outstanding."

"I take it you like the view."

"I do. I've never seen anything like it, except in photos, of course. Too bad it's so far away from everything."

Tom smiled to himself. She obviously thought of New York City as the center of the universe. "It's not so far away," he said dryly. "Matter of fact, it's right outside my front door."

"Well, yeah, but I—oh my God. Stop the truck."

Tom pulled over to the shoulder as she scrambled to unfasten her seat belt and opened the door.

"Are you feeling sick? I'll bet it's all those candy—"

"I'm fine." She nearly fell out of the truck before she

finally managed to climb around her gear and jump to the shoulder of the road. Shading her eyes with her hand, she gazed upward. "Come and look!"

Curious, he obliged, checking to make sure nobody was headed down the road behind them before he opened the door and got out.

"There." She pointed toward the blue sky.

He looked up, squinting a little. The large bird gliding above them was unmistakable, its seven-foot wingspan supported by the upward draft from the mountains, its white head and tail gleaming in the sun. His heart lifted every time he saw one.

"It's a bald eagle, isn't it?" she said in a hushed voice.

"Yep." Then he spotted the second one, the female of the pair, most likely. He touched her shoulder and pointed.

"There's his mate."

She clutched his arm. "Oh, Tom. They're...magnificent."

The catch in her voice caused him to look down at her, and sure enough, there were tears in her eyes. The sight of the bald eagles had stirred her in a way he understood all too well. For her, this was probably a first-time experience. He liked being around for that, just as he liked the way she'd grabbed his arm when she got excited.

"Well." She turned loose of his arm as the eagles soared out of sight and glanced at him. "Thanks. I've never seen an eagle before, except in the zoo."

"It's not quite the same."

Her smile was gentle "No, it's not quite the same."

In that moment Tom had his first premonition that this woman would become more than just another greenhorn visiting the Whispering Winds. He might not be interested in marriage anymore, but that didn't mean he'd given up on women altogether. An elemental connection tightened his gut. He made a practice of not getting involved with ranch guests, but this might be the time to make an exception.

3

CLEO HAD THOUGHT her decision to create a calendar featuring Montana cowboys had been pure marketing strategy, yet as the spectacular scenery unfolded with each bend in the road, she remembered an old childhood fantasy. She'd totally forgotten that one of her favorite pretend games had involved being a cowgirl living on a ranch surrounded by mountains. As Tom continued the drive to the Whispering Winds Ranch, he presented her with views of mountain meadows, streams and rose-colored bluffs right out of her youthful imagination.

Very few others shared the road with them, which surprised her. "Why is the traffic so light?" she asked finally.

"It's about normal for around here."

"But the road's practically deserted."

"You take eight hundred thousand people and spread them over a state the size of Montana, and you don't get much traffic."

"That's the state's population? But the city of New York has —"

"About ten times more people than the whole state of Montana. I'm well aware of that. I felt like a bull trapped in a rodeo chute whenever I went back there. Now, thank God, I don't have to go anymore."

"Are you kidding? New York is fantastic! Everywhere you look, there's something exciting to see."

"Not if you want to see this."

She had to concede his point. You couldn't find anything like Montana in Manhattan, but then she hadn't built her career on pretty pictures of mountain vistas and sparkling rivers, either. She gazed at the profile of the man beside her, and her trigger finger began to itch. She'd love to capture that decisive jawline, the curve of his ear, the aggressive line of his nose.

Her trusty thirty-five millimeter was loaded and ready inside her camera bag. She unzipped the bag slowly and eased the cap off the lens. Glancing down to check her settings, she lifted the camera out of the bag as noiselessly as possible.

"Don't." He hadn't moved his head even a fraction of an inch, yet he apparently knew what she was up to.

She put the lens cap back on. "What if I didn't use any of the photos for the calendar? What if I just took them for fun?"

"Don't forget, I was married to a model for five years, and I have some acquaintance with professional photographers. You don't usually shoot for fun."

She had to admit he was right. Although she enjoyed her work, she never took photos anymore just for the heck of it. No point in wasting time and film on something that wouldn't sell. "Okay, I wouldn't be doing it for the fun of it. I just think that if you saw what I could accomplish, you might change your mind about posing."

"Sorry. You'll have to find somebody with a bigger ego than mine if you want to succeed with that argument. I only look in the mirror so I won't nick myself when I shave."

Immediately she had a new idea for a shot—Tom, shirtless but wearing his Stetson, wielding a straight razor as he stood in front of a crockery washbasin. She'd love to know what he'd look like without a shirt. His open collar revealed a glimpse of chest hair that looked promising. Dammit, she wanted to get this man on film. She was so used to cooperative men that she was having a hard time with this one's refusal.

"Here we are," Tom said, swinging off the asphalt onto a dirt road. "Welcome to the Whispering Winds." He braked the truck to a stop in front of a metal gate and got out to open it. Barbed-wire fencing stretched into the distance on both sides of the gate, and wooden posts rose on either side of it. Suspended from a lodgepole that bridged the posts was a sign with Whispering Winds Ranch carved deep into the wood.

Tom climbed in, pulled the truck through and went back to close the gate, giving Cleo ample time to get the lay of the land. The road angled down to a wide meadow rimmed with evergreens and aspen. Beyond the meadow the terrain sloped upward as hills gave way to jagged, snowcapped mountain peaks.

It would have made a terrific postcard. Centered in the shot, if she were photographing the scene, was a log ranch house nestled against the trees. It reminded her of the Lincoln Log house she'd built as a kid during her cowgirl phase, and it had a weathered look that suggested it had been there for a long time. An aging barn and split-rail corrals occupied the right side of the meadow, and several rustic cabins clustered on the left. A string of riders appeared from among the trees and headed for the corrals, almost as if they'd been cued on stage when she arrived. To make the picture complete, a black-and-white dog ran out to greet the riders.

"This is *exactly* what I was looking for," Cleo said as Tom got back into the truck. "You don't mind if pieces of your ranch show up in my calendar, do you?"

"Pieces of my ranch are fine. Just no pieces of me." His gaze held no compromise. "And don't think I haven't heard of zoom lenses. Take a picture of me and use it without my permission and I'll haul your fanny into court."

She was highly insulted. "I wouldn't dream of it. That's unethical."

His answering laugh was short and humorless. "When I was married to Deidre, we had paparazzi on our tail a few times. Don't preach to me about the ethics of photographers."

That got to her. She prided herself on her ethics. "Just because you didn't like being married to a successful model doesn't give you the right to be so prejudiced against photographers in general."

He negotiated around a puddle in the road. "It does give me the right. I earned it the hard way."

"For your information, I always get permission from my subjects before using the photographs. So do all the photographers I know."

"Good. You can be sure I won't give it."

"I've never met someone so phobic in my life."

He didn't respond.

Cleo sighed. If she had any sense, she'd give up on him, but that cover-shot possibility was seared into her brain. Now she wouldn't be satisfied with the calendar until she'd nailed down her concept. Maybe she'd find another cowboy who would project the image she wanted, but probably not. Tom was a rare find, and she'd photographed enough men to realize it.

Tom stopped the truck as the string of five riders crossed the road in front of them.

The lead rider, a lanky cowboy Cleo estimated to be in his mid-twenties, changed direction and headed for the truck. "Just take them on into the corral, folks," he called out to the riders—a man, woman and two kids. "I'll be right there."

Tom rolled down the window as the cowboy drew alongside. "How's it going, Jeeter?"

"Saw some cat tracks up along Settlers Creek. Looks like a big one, maybe looking to pick off a calf or two."

Cleo gasped. "A cougar?"

The cowboy named Jeeter leaned down to peer into the cab. He touched the brim of his hat in salute. "A cougar for sure, ma'am."

"Jeeter Neff, meet Cleo Griffin, our photographer from New York City," Tom said.

"Pleased to meet you," Jeeter said. "Listen, Tom, maybe somebody oughta go after that cat before something happens."

Tom rested his forearms on the steering wheel and frowned.

"That's what your dad would have done," Jeeter said.

Tom sighed. "I know. But in his day we had more of those cats. We planned to rotate the herd to a different pasture next month, anyway. Let's do it earlier, and see if we can get them out of range."

"You're the boss."

"We can take some of the dudes, give them a cattle-drive experience." Tom turned to Cleo. "Maybe you'd like to go along and take this cat's picture if it shows up."

She had no desire to come face-to-face with predatory wildlife, but going on a cattle drive might give her valuable background for the calendar. "Sounds like an interesting idea," she said, assessing Jeeter with a practiced eye. He didn't have Tom's seasoned ruggedness, but his blond good looks and mustache would definitely satisfy some woman's fantasy. "I'm doing a calendar called *Montana Men,* and I'm here to photograph cowboys. Are you interested, Jeeter? "

"No joke?" Jeeter asked, pushing his hat back on his head. "You mean, I'd be like Mr. November or something?"

Cleo laughed. "I can't guarantee what month, but yes, something like that."

"Would I have to take off my clothes? I'm not saying I wouldn't do it, but I'd like to know beforehand."

"At the most, you'd only have to take off your shirt. I visualize the jeans as being part of the sex appeal."

'Yes, *ma'am!*" Jeeter grinned. "Just tell me where and when." He glanced at Tom. "That's if it's okay with you, Tom, and it fits into the schedule and everything."

"I'm sure we can work something out," Tom said, his tone dry.

"Are you gonna pose, Tom? I think you'd be—"

"No."

Jeeter gazed at his boss, then leaned down to look at Cleo again. "There's no catch to this, is there? Like I have to pay you, or something?"

"As a matter of fact, I'll pay you," Cleo said.

"If that don't beat all," Jeeter said. "I get to hang on

somebody's wall and be paid for the privilege. Well, I'd better go check on the dudes." He touched his hat brim again. "Just let me know when you want me, ma'am." He cantered away.

"You sure put a swash in his buckle," Tom said as he lifted his foot from the brake.

"I hate to tell you, but that's the reaction I usually get. You're the only man who's ever refused to pose for me."

"And I intend to hold on to that distinction."

"You don't think you're being just a little stubborn? A little prejudiced? A little pigheaded?"

"You aren't going to flatter me into it, either. I suggest you drop the subject, Cleo, or we won't have much to do with each other while you're here."

"You're being ridiculous."

"Pardon me, ma'am, but on my ranch, I'll be whatever I want to be."

"Which is, difficult," Cleo muttered.

"I prefer to think of myself as an independent thinker. Well, here we are." Tom parked the truck next to a lovely little cabin tucked into the trees and more secluded than the other five. Red tulips and yellow daffodils bloomed by the doorstep and eyelet curtains hung at the windows.

"Well, the accommodations certainly are charming," Cleo said pointedly.

Tom paused before opening his door. "I can be charming, too, if someone's not threatening to point a camera in my face."

She met his determined gaze and decided to retreat for the time being. "Understood," she said. She had two weeks to wear him down. One thing she'd learned early in this game was patience. She opened her door and started to climb out around her gear.

"If you'll hold on, I'll be more than happy to help you out, ma'am," he said, all brusqueness gone from his manner. "I wouldn't want you to fall and break that pretty neck of yours."

She turned to him and lifted her eyebrows.

"See?" He grinned. "Charming."

Well, he was, she had to admit. Her insides did a funny little dance in the warmth of that smile. "Thanks," she said. "I could use some help, at that."

"Coming right up." He hopped out and walked around to her side.

She handed him the backpack and he set it on the ground with no fuss, but the suitcase wedged between her knees was a more delicate matter. She had to spread her legs to make room to lift it out, and he kept brushing her inner thighs as he maneuvered it out of the cab. He acted as if he didn't notice, and she pretended not to, either, but her body noticed, all right. She grew very warm in certain strategic places, and her pulse rate skyrocketed.

This would never do. First of all, she wanted him as a subject for her calendar, which ruled out hanky-panky. Secondly, she had to save herself for the cowboy she'd ask to marry her while she was out here in the wilds of Montana. And that cowboy definitely wasn't Tom. He wasn't nearly docile enough for the role she had in mind.

"Are you about ready to come out of there, ma'am, or did you need a few more minutes to cogitate on the situation?"

She glanced over and found him watching her, his

mouth curved in a smile and his thumbs hooked casually through his belt loops. It would make an excellent
shot. She hoped to hell he hadn't been able to guess that
she'd been staring into space because his accidental
touch had turned her on. Grabbing her camera bag, she
scrambled to the ground.

Tom led the way into the cabin, which wasn't locked.
Cleo was fast learning that nobody bothered locking either house or car doors out here. That would take some
getting used to, after the triple-lock system and the se-
curity alarm she had for her Greenwich Village apartment.

The interior of the cabin matched the charm of the ex-
terior. The varnished log walls gave a honey-colored
glow to the furnishings, which included a king-size
bed, bureau and dressing table, all in whitewashed
pine. A turquoise coverlet on the bed, western art on the
walls and Indian-print rugs on the floor completed the
frontier look.

Cleo nodded in satisfaction. "This is great."

"It's my favorite cabin," Tom said, "on account of its
being back in the trees a little more. And then there's
the hot tub just out the back door."

"Hot tub?" Cleo frowned at the vision of some plastic
monster mucking up the rustic ambience of the place.

"The Whispering Winds is built on the site of natural
hot springs," Tom said. "Didn't you read the bro-
chure?"

"No, I left that to Bernie. She must have forgotten
about the hot springs."

"Come on. I'll show you." Tom left her suitcase and
backpack on the floor and walked back outside.

After some inner debate, Cleo left her camera bag

there, too, before following him out the door. Surely no one would sneak in and steal her camera while she was out inspecting the hot tub, yet leaving it in an open cabin bothered her anyway. Big-city living had built caution into her. She wondered what it must be like to worry about a cougar killing your calves instead of a drug-crazed psycho killing you. That was one aspect of city life she could do without.

She hurried to catch up with Tom, who was striding down a narrow path that disappeared into the trees. Her shoes crunched pine needles underfoot, and the dusky scent of sun-warmed underbrush tickled her nose. A couple of perky little birds chirped and fluttered in the branches of a tree near the path, and overhead a breeze passed through the evergreens with a sound like gentle surf—the whispering winds the ranch was named after, she concluded.

Tom seemed to walk with even more assurance now that his boots touched down on his own land. *On my ranch, I'll be whatever I want to be.* It was a great line, and she'd love to use it in the bio printed next to his calendar photo. The calendar photo that would also appear on the cover of *Montana Men,* she vowed silently.

He glanced over his shoulder. "This is our most private hot tub. Some folks are spooked to be off here by themselves, but the dogs will always alert you if anything's around."

"Like what?" A little thrill of fear shot through her.

"Well, skunks, of course, and raccoons and deer. We've had a cougar down this far once in my lifetime, a few moose, wolves once in a while. Oh, and there was that one time a grizz showed up."

"A grizzly bear?" Cleo glanced around and her heart

pounded faster. What had seemed like peaceful forest sounds took on a sinister cast. In her imagination, the crack of a twig became the warning of an approaching monster. "I thought they were all up in Alaska somewhere."

"We get a few down here now and then," Tom announced as if reporting on the migration of meadowlarks.

"When was the last time?"

"About five years ago." He stepped into a clearing where a redwood tub just right for two people bubbled away. "Here it is, a little bit of paradise."

"Unless a grizzly shows up." Cleo stepped forward to dip her hand into the warm water. After traveling all day, she'd like nothing better than to sink naked into it.

"The dogs would tell you if a bear was around." Tom trailed his hand through the water. "Unless the wind was wrong and they couldn't smell him, that is."

She glanced over at him. "Are you deliberately trying to scare me? Because you're doing a hell of a job."

His grin gave her the answer. "Okay, I'm laying it on a little thick. It's a bad habit I have with city people. You have a better chance of being mugged in New York than meeting a grizzly on this ranch."

"I don't find that a comforting comparison. I feel as if I should be armed with my canister of Mace."

Tom gave her a considering glance. "You know, all kidding aside, I can't remember the last time we've had a single woman as a guest. I didn't give much thought to the fact you might be scared staying out here alone. Maybe we should switch you over to the main house."

"I'd rather stay here." She'd already had fallen in love with her private little cabin. In addition to that, she really longed for a good long soak in this secluded hot tub, bears or no bears. "I'm sure pioneer women lived alone in the wilderness all the time."

"Modern-day women, too. My mother managed by herself lots of times when my dad and the hands went out on a roundup and took the cook along."

"This ranch used to belong to your parents?"

"And three generations before that. Mom and Dad would still be here running the place if Dad hadn't come down with Alzheimer's. They finally gave in and moved to Billings, where his specialist is located."

Five generations of McBrides on this spot. No wonder he looked so at home here. "Do you have brothers and sisters?"

"A sister. She fell in love with a Texan and moved to Austin."

The disbelief in his voice made Cleo smile. "Imagine that."

"Once she started a family, she lost interest in the ranch, so I bought her out."

"You really love the Whispering Winds, don't you?"

"It's home," he said quietly.

The warm water ran through Cleo's fingers as she remembered an essay she'd read in college about the importance of place in a person's life. She'd never understood the essay until now. Although she loved the city, she didn't feel the intense connection that Tom obviously felt to the ranch. He was different from the other men she'd known, including her father, who dedicated themselves to careers and business success. Curiosity had driven her to take up photography, and it drove her now—that and the hope that she would still get Tom to be part of her project.

"My time here is limited," she began, feeling her way toward the thought that was only half-formed in her mind. "I have a job to do, obviously, but while I'm here...I'd count it as a special favor if you'd show me what makes this place so special to you."

He contemplated her for a long moment. "I'd like that," he said at last. "Can you ride?"

"Some." She remembered English-riding lessons when she was ten, the struggle to win blue ribbons in competition and the sense of failure when all she could achieve was second place. She hadn't been on a horse since.

"Think you could handle a couple of days helping us move the cattle?" he said. "Tomorrow I have some chores to tend to, but the morning after that I'm planning to take a couple of hands and any guests who want to go. We'll see if we can get those calves out of harm's way."

"Sure." She'd never slept outside in her life, but cowboys did it all the time, and she was here to capture the spirit of being a cowboy. "I'll probably get some ideas for calendar shots."

"What you'll probably get is saddle-sore, if you haven't ridden much lately. But we'll take a wagon along with sleeping bags and grub, so if you get tired, you can ride in—"

"I'll keep up."

He rubbed his chin and gazed at her. "This isn't a test, Cleo. I'm sorry if I gave you the idea that dudes have to prove themselves out here. You're supposed to relax and have a good time."

"But I'm not on vacation."

He studied her. "And I'll bet you don't take vacations."

"Nope. And I'll bet you don't, either."

"Nope." He smiled. "But it's mighty pretty country up there among the pines, so maybe we could both pretend a little."

By God, he was flirting with her. She wondered if she could entice him to participate in her calendar project with some innocent flirtation without compromising her principles. It would be tricky. "Okay, we'll pretend we're on vacation. But tomorrow I have to work. Can I borrow Jeeter for a couple of hours?"

"You can. I wouldn't want to stand in the way of his fame and fortune."

"You're free to watch me work if you're curious. You might change your mind about posing."

"I've seen photo shoots before, and I won't change my mind."

The challenge in his voice quickened her pulse and hardened her resolve. "We'll see."

Tom was sailing on uncharted waters. As he stood by the hot tub and looked at Cleo, the sunlight filtering through the pine branches lighting up the gold in her hair, desire stirred in him with sweet persistence. He really shouldn't be having such thoughts about one of his guests, but he'd never had a guest quite like this one, either.

As he'd told Cleo, single women were a rarity at the ranch, with couples and families making up the biggest part of the guest roster. Years ago, two widows got in the habit of booking several weeks at the ranch each summer, but those sixty-something ladies were a far cry from a woman like Cleo. As he stood alone with her in this peaceful clearing, he fought the urge to step closer and snug up the line of tension between them. With a few well-chosen words and any encouragement from her, he might even risk taking her in his arms.

He wondered what she'd do. Push him away, most likely. Or maybe not. The interest she'd shown so far hinted that she might lift that full mouth to his. He probably should think the notion through a little more before he acted on it, though. A similar notion about a New York City woman had turned into major heartache. This one wanted to take his picture, and she might even be thinking that flirtation was a way to accomplish her ends.

"I'd better get to that paperwork I mentioned," he said. "Unless you need any help getting settled in."

Awareness flashed in her eyes.

He held his breath, wondering if she'd take him up on his offer. Now that he'd thrown out the comment, he wondered if it would be wise to follow through so quick. Reason told him it wouldn't be.

"No, I'll be fine," she said at last.

He let out his breath and discovered he was more disappointed than he'd expected under the circumstances. "I'll be going, then."

"Okay. By the way, when's dinner?"

He smiled. This constant appetite of hers amused him. "At six, up at the house. We eat family style in the dining room."

"Speaking of all the families around here, is there a rule about wearing a bathing suit in the hot tub? I wouldn't want to embarrass anyone."

The rope of tension linking them snapped tight again.

Unless he missed his guess, she wanted him to know she planned to skinny-dip in the tub. He got the picture, and it scrambled his brains all the more. "The families don't use this one," he said. "Cabin six is set up for couples, and the private hot tub is part of the deal. You might want to wait until after dark, though, just to be on the safe side."

Cleo cupped water in her hand and let it run through her fingers. "Thanks. I'll keep that in mind."

"See you at dinner." He started out of the clearing.

"That's not the path we came in on," she called after him.

He paused and turned to her. "No. It's a shortcut to the house."

"So there are two paths leading to this clearing, one from the cabin and one from the main house?"

"That's right."

"Is that because you use this hot tub when nobody's staying in the cabin?"

"I've been known to."

"Maybe we can work out a system so we can share it."

Hellfire. This woman promised to be a handful, that is if he decided to take the considerable gamble of finding out. "Maybe so. Well, see you at dinner." He touched the brim of his hat and got himself out of there before he said or did something he wouldn't be able to take back. He'd like to share that hot tub with her, all right. Besides, if they decided to play games in the bubbling mineral water, he could be pretty sure she wouldn't have her damn camera hanging around her neck.

4

WIND GUSTS scented with rain pulled at Cleo's hair as she walked up to the main house for dinner. Clouds sat on the jagged crust of the mountains like scoops of blueberry ice cream, and the temperature had dropped by at least fifteen degrees. Even a greenhorn could tell a storm was on the way, Cleo thought, which probably doused her plans for a hot-tub experience tonight.

She was angry with herself for her part in the hot-tub discussion with Tom. His refusal to be part of her project stung, but she hoped a devilish sense of revenge was all that had motivated her to blurt out her intention of hot tubbing naked. She'd hate to think that she was unscrupulous enough to suggest sexual favors in exchange for his photo in her calendar, favors she'd never deliver. She wanted him on the cover, but she wouldn't sacrifice her character to get him there.

The sound of hammering drew her gaze to the roof of the two-story house, and there was Tom, kneeling to work on what must be a loose shingle. He wore no hat, and the wind whipped at his sun-streaked hair. Behind him rose the mountains and the darkening clouds. In his concentration on the task, she glimpsed the spirit of his pioneer ancestors, tough folks who had stood up to a tough country and won the right to live here.

She cupped her hands over her mouth. "Soup's on!"

He stopped hammering and looked down at her. "I'll

eat later. This flapping's been driving Juanita, our cook, crazy, and I promised her I'd fix it before the next storm hit. That should be shortly."

She hadn't realized how much she'd counted on seeing him during the meal until the prospect was taken away. "What do people do around here for fun in the evenings?" she asked.

He leaned his hammer arm on his bent knee. "Go to bed."

Had a New Yorker said that to her, she would have immediately got the double meaning, as intended, but Tom probably meant exactly what he'd said and nothing more. Being a city girl, and a sexually frustrated one, at that, she heard those simple words and immediately placed herself in a rumple of sheets and blankets with a certain rancher while the rain poured down outside. She really had to find a docile cowboy and get hitched, as they said in the Wild West.

"I just thought maybe there would be line-dancing lessons or something," she said.

"There's a ranch down the road that has all that. I could get Jeeter or someone to take you. Folks that book here prefer it quiet in the evenings."

"So they can hear the bears coming."

He grinned at her. "That's right. Now you'd better get in there. Juanita doesn't like people coming late to her table, and I know you want to get on her good side."

She'd been stalling, just to have an excuse to be around him, as if she were a teenager with a crush on the star football player. That was sickening behavior for a woman, and she vowed to stop it immediately. "Happy hammering," she called, and walked into the house without another glance at the roof. There were other cowboys on the range, and soon she'd have a baker's dozen from which to choose a man to ease her ache.

The main living area of the house was deserted, with all the noise coming from a doorway off to the right which led into the dining room. Although the aroma of food drew her, Cleo's artistic eye would never let her race through a room as interesting as this one.

The decor was more sensuous than she would have expected, a stimulating blend of masculine and feminine aspects. A native-rock fireplace with a rough-hewn mantel dominated one end of the room, and the scent of wood smoke and pipe tobacco hung in the air. The rugged ambience was balanced by overstuffed leather couches so plump they begged to be enjoyed. She ran a hand over the arm of the one nearest her and felt a jolt of pleasure at the butter-soft texture.

What fun it would be to roll around on one of these couches with— Cleo stopped herself with a grimace. She needed to get her plan up and running and she needed to do it in a hurry, before she embarrassed herself.

A short, sturdy Hispanic woman wearing a food-stained apron came to the dining-room door. "Are you going to eat?" she asked.

"Yes, please." Cleo started toward the dining room. "You must be Juanita."

"And you're the photographer."

"That's right."

Juanita assessed her with dark eyes. "Tom said you brought a bunch of candy bars with you." It sounded like an indictment.

Thanks, Tom. "I like to eat at irregular times, and I didn't want to bother you."

Juanita looked her up and down. "If you keep eating candy bars, instead of good food, you won't keep that figure for long."

Cleo tried to keep from smiling. If Juanita's figure was an indication of what good food could do to a person's figure, Cleo was better off with her candy bars. "I suppose you're right, but I honestly don't like bothering anyone when I want something to eat, and Tom said you didn't like to have people messing around in your kitchen when you're not there."

"Well, Tom's right. If I started letting the dudes, I mean the guests, go in there whenever they wanted, I'd have nothing but trouble."

"I don't want to louse up your program, and the candy bars will do just—"

"I could make you a deal."

Cleo looked at her in surprise. "What kind of deal?"

"I have two little ones, Rosa and Peter, and they're growing up so fast. My mother and father in Mexico are begging me for pictures, but I'm no good with a camera. If you'd take some special ones that I could send as Christmas presents, you can come into my kitchen and fix yourself whatever snacks you want."

"I don't usually take pictures of kids." Cleo didn't even know where she'd start.

Juanita waved her hand in a dismissive gesture. "I know. You take pictures of hunks. I have one of your calendars on my wall right now, the one with the construction guys on it." She winked. *"Muy bueno."*

It was a moment Cleo had never experienced before—meeting a stranger who had bought one of her calendars. The sales figures had been numbers to her, not people. She felt gratified, but a little self-conscious. "Thanks."

"You can do a fine job with Rosa and Peter. Now come on in and eat dinner before everything gets cold." Juanita turned and started back into the dining room, as if the matter was settled.

Cleo shrugged and followed her. She'd have to remember to tell Bernie about this when she called her tomorrow. Her friend would get a kick out of it, the sophisticated Cleo Griffin snapping shots of rug rats.

TOM HAD TROUBLE getting to sleep that night. As he lay in bed, most of his thoughts involved excuses for checking on Cleo. The storm battered the ranch with enough force to scare a New York woman, he reasoned, and he wasn't absolutely sure her cabin didn't leak.

Finally he got up and went to the bedroom window. From his vantage point on the second floor, he could see one end of Cleo's cabin, and her light was still on. He hadn't left her with any buckets, so she might be frantically trying to find containers for drips. He'd never installed phones in the cabins, so of course she wouldn't have a way to call the main house if she had problems.

Then logic prevailed. Luann, his extremely efficient head housekeeper, would have reported any evidence of a leak when she mentioned the stopped-up toilet. In fact, he would have noticed stains on the floor when he was in the cabin fixing the toilet. The roof was secure.

He went back to bed and closed his eyes, but he was still too revved up to sleep. He listened to the storm blow itself out, and got up again to see if Cleo's light still shone from the window. It did, beckoning him with her presence, creating a restlessness he hadn't felt in some time.

Standing naked in the darkness staring out the window, he imagined how the yipping of coyotes and the rattle of raccoons trying to pry off garbage-can lids might frighten somebody who'd never heard them before. He should probably go down there and make sure she was okay.

Before he finished dressing, he reversed the process and took off his clothes again. He was too damn eager, and that meant trouble. That meant she might turn out to be more than a casual fling, and casual flings were all he was in the market for these days. Once upon a time he might have figured that a New York woman was a perfectly safe bet for a brief affair. Now he knew himself better.

If he started something with Cleo tonight, she'd have two weeks to burrow under his skin. It would be more than enough time to screw up his life but good. If he intended to get involved with her at all, he'd better pace himself so that before he started to fall for her, she'd be long gone.

He disciplined himself to take slow, deep breaths, and finally found sleep, but sleep also meant dreams. Dawn greeted him with an erection that required a cold shower before he could pull on his jeans. Impatient with himself, he headed down to help Jeeter and Stan with the morning feeding, and wished that his first thought hadn't been whether Cleo would make it to breakfast.

Sometime later, as he was on his second cup of coffee, he concluded that she wasn't going to show up. The other guests had come and gone, leaving Juanita and

Luann to the cleanup chores in the big sunny dining room. Tom had checked with all of the dudes to find out who wanted to go on the cattle drive tomorrow, and he'd had five takers—one young childless couple and another couple with a fourteen-year-old daughter.

Now he sat alone at one end of the room's twin trestle tables and lingered over his coffee. He had no business taking it easy on this fine June morning, not with the amount of work to be done today, but he wanted to see Cleo again, if only for a moment.

Just as he was about to give up and tackle his list of chores, Cleo came through the double doors to the dining room looking like a zombie. A beautiful blond zombie, but a zombie nonetheless.

Juanita stopped wiping the table she'd just cleared and glanced up.

Tom braced himself for the tirade. Juanita considered tardiness at mealtime a personal insult, and it didn't matter if the offender was a paying guest or not. Fortunately, the Whispering Winds had a lot of return customers, and most everyone took Juanita's dictatorial ways in stride because she cooked like a goddess.

Juanita put down her dishcloth and walked over to Cleo. "You look like you could use a cup of coffee, *querida*." She cupped Cleo's elbow and guided her to the bench at Tom's table. "Sit here and I'll bring you some. How about some toast? A soft-boiled egg?"

Tom's mouth hung open in amazement.

"Toast and black coffee is all I need, Juanita. Thanks so much." Cleo slid onto a bench and glanced down the table toward Tom. "Do mornings always come this early around here?"

Tom closed his mouth. "Generally speaking." That

sleepy-eyed look of hers registered on his libido. He imagined waking up next to her and gradually, patiently kissing that sleepiness away.

Juanita bustled in with a steaming mug. "Here you go. Toast is on the way."

Tom was staring at Juanita in amazement, but she ignored him and hurried back out of the room.

"Thanks, Juanita," Cleo called after her. Then she took a long sip of coffee and closed her eyes.

"Are you all right?"

"I'm getting there." Her eyes drifted open again and she took another swallow of coffee. "My brain will start functioning any second now. I swear to God I heard a rooster crowing outside my window."

"That would be Rooster Cogburn. He pretty much has the run of the place and he does tend to crow when it gets light out. That's a rooster's job."

"I don't suppose you could give him a few days off? Send him to visit his brother in L.A. or something?"

"You're not a morning person."

"Doesn't look like it, does it?" She drank more coffee. "How was your night?"

"Noisy."

He snorted. "Compared to New York with all the sirens and constant traffic? Are you kidding?"

"But I'm used to those noises. Here there's quiet, and then howling, and quiet, and then rustling, then more quiet, and yipping. Howling, rustling, yipping. Rustling, yipping, howling. All night long. I felt like I was sleeping on a bench at the Bronx Zoo."

"I wondered if I should check on you."

She looked more alert. "You did?"

"But then I decided a New York chick like you wouldn't be scared."

"I didn't say I was scared. Just awake."

Juanita swept back into the room. "Here's your toast, and some homemade apple jelly." She set a plate and a crock of jelly in front of Cleo and poured her some more coffee.

"This looks just fine. I appreciate it. And the coffee's great."

"If you want anything else, just call me." Juanita patted Cleo on the shoulder before starting back toward the kitchen.

"Hold it," Tom said. "If I may be so bold as to ask, what exactly is going on here?"

Juanita turned to him, the coffee carafe in one hand.

"I'm serving our guest a little breakfast. Isn't that what you hired me for?"

"Yeah, but you've never let anybody else get away with coming in late for a meal, unless it's some sort of emergency. And you're treating Cleo like...like Cleopatra on her barge, for God's sake."

"This woman is an artist," Juanita said disparagingly. "She can't be expected to live by the same schedule as the rest of us."

Tom looked down the table at Cleo, who was trying to hide a smile behind her coffee mug. He gazed at her for several seconds. "I see."

"I'll be back with a coffee refill in a little while, Cleo." Juanita started out of the room.

"I could use a coffee refill about now, myself," Tom called over his shoulder.

Juanita paused.

"If you can spare the time."

Juanita walked over and poured coffee into his mug. "Are you going to pose for her?"

"No, I'm not." He took a sip from his mug.

Juanita studied him for a moment. "I guess you're a little old for it."

He choked on his coffee. Thirty-eight wasn't old. Men hit their prime at his age, and he'd never felt better, more alive, more ready for...well, that wasn't the point. He cleared his throat. "As a matter of fact, she asked me."

"He turned you down?" she asked Cleo.

"Flat." Cleo had perked up considerably in the past few minutes and looked delighted with the conversation.

"Why on earth would he do that?" Juanita turned to him, her expression disbelieving. "You might not be the most handsome man in the world, but you're not bad for a cowhand. I'll bet she could make you look even better."

"As flattered as I am by that speech, Juanita, I'd rather clean the chicken coop with a toothbrush."

Juanita shrugged. "Some people wouldn't know a golden opportunity if it bit them in the backside."

"I guess not," Cleo said. "Thanks for breakfast."

"Anytime." Juanita left the room shaking her head.

"You've cast a spell on my cook," Tom said when Juanita was out of earshot.

Cleo laughed. "Apparently. Want to know my secret?"

"I imagine everyone in the county would like to know your secret. Juanita's the best cook in these parts, and she knows it. Why she hangs around the Whispering Winds is a mystery, except that I let her do whatever she wants. She doesn't dance to anyone's tune, but you seem to have her wrapped around your little finger."

"My trigger finger, to be more exact. She wants me to take pictures of her kids." Cleo bit into the toast and murmured her approval.

"Oh." Tom watched with pleasure as she sank her teeth into the crunchy bread and swiped her tongue over a spot of jelly that landed on her lower lip. "That makes sense. She dotes on those kids."

Cleo swallowed the bite of toast. "Where's the dad?"

"The marriage didn't work out, but they're both staunch Catholics, so divorce wasn't an option. He's on the rodeo circuit and stops by every month or so to see the kids, but she's pretty much on her own. She's hired a teenage girl to watch them when she's busy in the kitchen."

"Sounds like a difficult situation," Cleo said.

"It is."

"But she strikes me as pretty tough. And damn, she makes good coffee." Cleo took another long drink.

Tom wondered how long he could put off work without somebody coming to look for him. He was having a great time sharing this slice of morning with Cleo. "Juanita's tough, all right. I thought she was going to punch out Deidre once."

"Really? Did Deidre insult her cooking?"

"No. They...let's just say that Juanita didn't approve of Deidre's behavior." Deidre had imagined Juanita would back her on the abortion question, that they'd unite as two women who both faced the problems created by men. Deidre had miscalculated on that one.

Cleo gazed at him over her coffee mug. He figured she wanted to ask what behavior had caused Juanita to consider violence toward his ex-wife, but she held back. He probably shouldn't have brought up the subject, but the warm sun through the windows, the taste of Juanita's coffee and the quiet that had settled over the dining room all combined to give him the relaxed impression that he could tell her anything at all and she would understand. Still, Deidre's abortion wasn't the sort of topic you threw out to someone you'd known less than twenty-four hours.

With a sigh of regret, he pushed himself away from the table and stood. "I'd better get going."

"What's on the schedule for you today?"

He liked the feeling of having someone—someone soft and feminine—ask the question. He'd had an image of marriage that never came quite true with Deidre. They didn't spend enough time together to fall into a routine, and he'd discovered routine was comforting to him.

He adjusted his hat, a newer Stetson than the one he'd worn for her benefit yesterday. "Some repair work on the barn this morning, and we're breeding one of our mares this afternoon."

Her cheeks grew a shade pinker. "Really? Will it be one of those artificial insemination jobs?"

"No, we don't get that fancy around here. For the few times we get involved in the process, the old-fashioned way is good enough." He wondered if the conversation was affecting her the way it was affecting him. "You're going to take pictures of Jeeter today, aren't you?"

"We're scheduled for right after lunch, probably in the barn. I'm going to scout out some locations this morning. I'll make sure we don't get in the way of your...breeding."

"That's not until two-thirty. A neighbor's bringing his stallion over then."

"Love in the afternoon," Cleo said.

"It's not what I'd call love."

"Lust, then."

"That's closer, I guess. I sometimes feel sorry for animals. We can manipulate them so easily because of their biology." While *he* was so much more sophisticated, he thought. Sure he was. That's why he was picturing Cleo on her back in a pile of hay, wearing nothing but a smile. "Stop by the corral if you want, after your photography session," he said.

"Stop by the barn if you want, before your breeding session," she countered, putting down her mug and standing.

"We'll see." He glanced at her plate. "You'd better get some more toast or something before you go. I doubt that will hold you until lunch."

She grinned at him. "You forget. It doesn't have to."

"Oh yeah." He rubbed the back of his neck. "I still can't believe all it took was a camera to make Juanita your devoted servant."

"A camera's a powerful tool."

"I guess you're right. You probably know that Native Americans used to believe it stole your spirit."

"I'd heard that." Her gaze was searching. "You halfway believe it yourself, don't you?"

He paused to think about the concept. At last he nodded. "Yeah, Cleo, I do. See you around."

5

CLEO MUNCHED her way through the morning, dropping by the kitchen several times to pilfer snacks. In the process she met Rosa, aged four, and Peter, aged two, when the baby-sitter brought them in for lunch. Cleo had no idea how she'd go about photographing the dark-eyed cherubs when the time came, but Juanita was so entranced with the idea that Cleo pretended more confidence than she felt.

Her morning snacking made her own lunch unnecessary, so while the hands and guests were inside the ranch house eating, Cleo took advantage of the deserted barn to set up for the photo session with Jeeter. During the morning, she'd figured out that light filtering through the big double doors would give her enough to shoot without a flash, which she preferred. Using ambient light instead of flashes or strobes was one of her trademarks, and she was vain about it.

Just inside the door the light fell just the way she wanted, and she positioned a bale of hay up against the weathered side of a vacant stall. All the stalls were empty on this warm summer day, now that the horses had been turned out to graze. Cleo wondered where the mare of the hour had been taken and if she was having her hooves painted and her mane curled for her big date. Cleo was dying with curiosity about the event, but she'd heard that watching such goings-on had an effect on the humans, and she didn't need any more of that certain effect, thank you very much.

With the horses gone from the barn, only a tortoise-shell cat and her newborn kittens remained to keep Cleo company as she arranged the hay bale and checked the light from different angles. She discovered the little family nestled inside a wooden box behind a hand cart. The saddle blanket tucked in the box looked deliberately placed there. Somebody had provided this kitten nursery, Cleo decided, and wondered if Tom was that much of a softie.

The scent of hay, oats and horses brought back bitter-sweet memories of her English-riding days. She'd loved the horses and had wanted one of her own. Her father had told her he'd buy her the horse of her dreams after she won her first blue ribbon. A man of his word, her father. She never got her horse.

Jeeter arrived right on time, interrupting her thoughts. Polished spurs jingling, he clomped into the barn wearing what she suspected was his Saturday-night going-to-town outfit—new jeans, ostrich-skin boots, a wildly patterned western shirt, a leather vest and a black Stetson that looked fresh out of the box.

He touched the brim in greeting. "Ma'am."

"Don't you look fine, Jeeter."

"I'm as nervous as a bull at cuttin' time," he admitted.

She figured out that he was referring to the practice of castrating cattle. "Don't worry," she said. "This photo session will have the opposite effect. You'll be strutting around like Rooster Cogburn when it's over. The guys tell me it's very good for the ego." She pulled a small notebook out of her camera bag. "Before we start, I need a little background on you."

"Nothin' much to tell."

"Oh, I doubt that." She ran through her routine questions about age, birthplace, work experience and hobbies. Then she casually tossed in one tailored for this project alone. "Do you have a girlfriend?"

"How come you need to know that?"

Cleo had her answer ready. "I'd like to give her a complimentary copy of the calendar."

Jeeter grinned. "I don't know about that. A picture of me is okay, but I don't think I want Julie gawking at all those other guys for the rest of the year."

So he had a girlfriend. Cleo hadn't really expected him to make the cut as husband material, but this detail settled it. She wouldn't horn in on another woman's territory. "Then maybe she'd like a framed copy of the picture I use in the calendar."

"That would be great. I could sign it, and everything."

"You bet. Well, let's get started."

Jeeter smoothed his blond mustache and fiddled with a button on his vest. "Is this what I should be wearing? I wasn't sure."

"You look terrific." She gazed straight into his blue eyes as she spoke. "Did anyone ever tell you you're the spitting image of Alan Jackson?"

"A time or two." He stood a little taller, and the gleam in his eyes became a little brighter.

"Let's start with you sitting on that bale of hay over there," she said.

"Yes, ma'am." Perched self-consciously on the edge

of the bale in his brand-new, totally buttoned-up clothes, he looked anything but sexy and relaxed.

In Cleo's experience, most guys started a session this way. After all, they weren't professional models, and they usually posed stiffly and stared straight at the camera as if they were having their picture taken at the driver's-license bureau. Her job was to get them to loosen up. She might waste an entire roll of film doing that, but if she succeeded, the second roll would be pure gold.

"That's nice," she said, looking through the viewfinder. "Lean back against the stall a little. Good." She clicked the shutter, knowing she wouldn't use the shot. "Now unbutton your vest."

Jeeter complied.

"You have a great build. Do you work out?" She snapped off a few more frames.

"Nope. Just regular cowboying." He pulled in his stomach and rolled his shoulders back.

Cleo had discovered that praising a man's body did wonders for the resulting photography. Fortunately, she didn't have to fake that praise. She loved looking at a well-built man, both as an artist and as a woman. "It's a shame to hide that physique. Let's try a few shots with the vest off."

"Yes, ma'am." His voice vibrated with sexual confidence now.

"And undo about four snaps on your shirt." She waited until he'd finished and was looking at her. Then she slowly licked her lips. "*Very* nice," she said, keeping her voice low and intimate. "Julie's a lucky woman."

"I'll tell her you said so."

"By all means." Cleo edged a little closer. "Lean down on your elbow and prop your boot on the hay. Mmm. I like that. I like that very much." Her implication, and men never failed to get it, was that she was enjoying the way the pose emphasized the bulge in their pants.

Jeeter's bulge stirred, and his breath was coming faster. "How about the shirt?" he said, his voice husky. "Do you want that off?"

"Unsnap it all the way and pull it out of the waistband," she murmured, clicking away. "We'll see what that looks like. Oh, I like that. As if you've just started to undress, just started the seduction. Cock your hips a little. What lovely muscles, Jeeter," she crooned, moving and clicking as she found different angles. "Look at me. Ah, that's perfect."

She might get what she wanted in the first roll, after all, she thought. His pupils were already dilated with sexual excitement, and there was a fine sheen of moisture on his bare chest.

"You must drive your girlfriend wild," she whispered. "You make her crazy with desire, don't you, Jeeter? You don't have to tell me. I know. Any woman who looks into your eyes would know."

His lips parted as he stared at her, thoroughly aroused and mesmerized by the sound of her voice. The problem was, she'd aroused herself in the process. It couldn't be helped, but it had to be controlled.

Yet she needed to feed this emotion building in him, because that was what women were looking for when they bought her calendars. "You're a fantastic lover, aren't you, Jeeter? You know how to please a woman so she can't get enough of you and your magnificent body."

He groaned softly.

"That's it," she said. "That's what I want. Give me what I want." She clicked the shutter rapidly, capturing the intensity before she ran out of film. Such a moment would never be sustained through reloading. She came to the end of the roll satisfied that she had her calendar shot. Sometimes, on a good day, it happened that way.

Slowly she straightened and brought the camera down. "That was fantastic, Jeeter."

"That's all?" His voice was rough with unexpressed passion.

"That should do it. You were wonderful." She turned to get the contract she'd tucked into her camera bag and saw Tom leaning in the doorway. In her current state, six feet of magnificent cowboy backlit by the sun was a powerful aphrodisiac. "Well, hello there."

"Hello, yourself." He didn't change position, just kept looking at her.

She thought it was encouraging that he'd been curious enough to come to the barn while she was shooting. She had to walk toward him to reach her camera bag. "How much of the session did you see?"

"Enough."

"Hey, boss," Jeeter said. "This is a real painless way to earn some cash."

"I imagine it is, Jeeter."

Cleo couldn't read his mood from his expression or the tone of voice, both of which seemed guarded. "Has the...uh...breeding started?"

"Not yet."

"Good." She swallowed. "I'd like to see how that's done."

"All right."

She leaned down and tucked her camera in the bag before pulling the contract out of a side pocket. "We're just about finished here."

"Take your time. They won't start anything until I get there."

"Okay." She turned and walked over to Jeeter, who was putting on his vest. "Here's the contract. I encourage you to take it home for the night and read everything. If you want a lawyer to see it, that's fine."

Jeeter straightened his vest and took the contract. "Or I could just sign it now and get it over with."

Tom spoke up. "Don't sign a contract until you've read it, Jeeter. You need to know what you've agreed to."

"I could read it back to front and not know what I'd agreed to, boss. That legal mumbo jumbo confuses the heck out of me."

Tom walked over to him. "Want me to take a look at it for you?"

"I'd be much obliged." He handed him the contract. "Say, boss, do you need me around here for anything in particular for the next couple of hours?"

"Any trail rides going out this afternoon?"

"Nope."

"Then I guess I don't have anything in particular for you to do. But I can always find—"

"I'd appreciate a couple of hours off." Jeeter tried to look nonchalant and failed. "Thought I'd ride over and see Julie."

Tom glanced at Cleo and back at Jeeter. "Yeah, go ahead, Ace."

"Thanks, boss." Jeeter turned to Cleo. "I'll get to see those pictures, right?"

"Of course. But I get the choice of which one to use."

"Don't forget about the one for Julie. And my mom might want one, too."

"We can talk about that." Cleo was careful about letting too many prints circulate. She wanted the pictures of her calendar boys to be unique. But sometimes she made exceptions for girlfriends and mothers.

"Yes, ma'am." Jeeter touched the brim of his hat. "It's been a pleasure." Then he left the barn with a decided swagger in his walk.

Cleo chuckled once he was out of earshot. "I think Julie just got lucky."

"And what if there had been no Julie?" Tom asked quietly.

Cleo glanced up into gray eyes that smoldered in a way that made her already keyed-up system kick into high gear. "That would be Jeeter's problem," she said. "I'm sure he would have found a way to take care of it."

"With you?"

She almost slapped him before she realized he didn't know about her code of ethics. After what he'd just seen, he couldn't be blamed for thinking she'd follow through on the seduction she'd begun if a man was single and available. "I have a rule. I don't sleep with my subjects."

He stepped closer. "Never?"

"Never." God, how she wanted him. Here. Now. On the floor of this barn, against that bale of hay. Anywhere. But that would ruin her cover plans, not to mention her husband hunt.

His voice rumbled low. "You get them all worked up and then leave them that way?"

She shrugged, trying to act as if her pulse wasn't beating a mile a minute just having him stand so close, teasing her with the scent of leather and sun and potent male. "It's no different for actors. They get all hot and bothered when they play love scenes, but they don't necessarily follow through with that behavior."

"Some do."

"Well, I don't. It's a reputation I'm proud of, and I intend to keep things that way."

"And what about you?"

She trembled at his caressing tone. "What about me?"

"How do you take care of all that tension boiling in that ripe body of yours?"

She swallowed. "What makes you think I'm affected at all?"

"Oh, I don't know." His glance flicked over her. "Maybe it's the scent of sex in the air. Maybe it's that look in your eyes that says you want a man's hands on you."

"Your enormous ego is working overtime."

"Is it?" He reached up and stroked a finger across her lower lip.

She gasped and stepped back.

"I didn't think so," he said.

"You surprised me."

"Then let's see how you react when you're not surprised." Tossing his hat and Jeeter's contract on the bale of hay, he closed the short distance between them and cupped her face in both hands.

She tried to draw away, but his touch was like rain falling on a parched field. She drank it in and wanted more, even though she knew it was a mistake. "No," she whispered as his head lowered.

"It's okay. I'm not one of your subjects."

"But I want you...to be."

"No way, baby." The touch of his lips was gentle, exploratory, tender.

Without warning, Cleo's restraint cracked wide open and she became the aggressor, clutching his head and deepening the kiss. He caught fire instantly, shifting the angle of his head for greater access and thrusting his tongue into her mouth.

The taste of him drove her wild. She matched him breath for ragged breath, sucking, licking, devouring what she needed, what they both needed. He pulled her close and she moaned at the full body contact. The man knew how to use his hands, and moisture rushed between her thighs as the ache to have him became almost unbearable.

Before she realized it, he'd backed her up against a rough wood wall and wrenched down the zipper of her jeans. His mouth was at her throat, his fingers unfastening her belt. Dimly, she realized he meant to take her, here in the barn.

"No!" The hoarse protest barely made it past her lips. "I don't want this." Her words were choked.

He paused and lifted his head to gaze into her eyes. He was panting. "The hell you don't."

"I don't." Summoning every reserve she had, she pushed him away.

He stared at her, chest heaving, the fly of his jeans stretched to the max. "You're a lousy liar, Cleo."

"I'm not lying. Once something like this happens between us, I can't use you for the cover of my calendar."

"Sweetheart, you can't use me anyway. Get over it and let us both have some relief."

She lifted her chin. "I'm not giving up. You'll pose for me before I leave."

"So you can treat me the way you just treated poor Jeeter?"

"It's business, Tom! Everyone benefits. It's the way I work."

"Well, you're not working that way with me." He turned away and propped his hands on his hips while he took several deep breaths. "Fasten your clothes. I have something you need to see."

She zipped her jeans and noticed he'd undone a couple of buttons on her blouse, too. She'd been so carried away she hadn't even known what he was doing. Her whole body ached and dripped with need, but she couldn't allow base instinct to rule her. Not if, by denying herself, she had a chance at a photo that would be the crown jewel in her career.

While she was straightening her clothes, he walked over and picked up his hat. He dusted it off and replaced it firmly on his head before picking up Jeeter's contract. He started flipping through it, paused and gave a low whistle.

"What?" she asked.

"I guess you do pay well."

"Of course." She wondered if money would make a difference to him. She had no idea of his financial situation, but unless he was independently wealthy, the money might come in handy. "And the amount is negotiable in your case, considering we're talking about a cover shot."

He glanced up from the contract. "I'm not doing it, Cleo." His smile beckoned to her. "And the sooner you accept that, the sooner we can get down to some good old-fashioned sex."

"I'm not interested."

"I think we just demonstrated how very interested you are."

"I mean mentally."

He laughed. "Making love isn't brain work. It's body work. Park your brain and have some fun with me, lady."

"No can do." She swung her camera bag to her shoulder. "A relationship with you would louse up...several things." She wasn't about to tell him that she was looking for a husband on this trip and didn't plan to settle for a brief affair. "Shall we go?"

"Absolutely. It's time for a little sex education." He folded the contract and tucked it in his hip pocket.

His comment, combined with the way the folded contract drew her gaze to his tight buns, had a predictable effect. Her nipples tightened and a warming trend began once again in her pelvic region. "Maybe this isn't such a great idea," she said as they started out of the barn. "I need to check and see if I have an overnight delivery from Bernie, anyway, and—"

"You don't. I would have found that out at lunch, because an overnight delivery out here in the country is a big deal. Nobody mentioned it."

"Oh. Well, speaking of lunch, I missed it because of the photo shoot, and I'm hungry."

He slanted a sideways glance at her as they walked side by side. "I'd say so. In fact, I'd say you were plum starved."

A flush warmed her cheeks. "Right after a photo shoot is a very vulnerable time for me. When you showed up, I just...reacted."

"Yes, ma'am, you sure did."

"It doesn't mean anything."

"If you say so."

"Now, if you'll excuse me, I'm going to the kitchen and find myself something to eat."

"Nope." Tom took her firmly by the arm and guided her toward the corral.

"What are you doing?" She tried to pull away from him, but his fingers remained clamped over her biceps like a manacle. "Tom, I said I've changed my mind about watching this little show. Let me go. I don't want to cause a scene."

"Neither do I. But after watching you with Jeeter, I think it's important for you to see what's about to happen in the corral. It should give you a better idea of why I won't pose for your calendar."

"My calendar? What on God's green earth would a couple of horses making whoopee have to do with my calendar?"

His smile was grim. "More than you think."

"Obviously," she muttered, but decided to go along, after all. If watching this spectacle would give her more insight into what made Tom tick, so much the better. "All right, I'll go with you."

"Good." He seemed to have forgotten that he still had a firm hold on her arm as they headed for the corral.

"You can turn me loose, Tom. I promise I won't bolt."

"Too bad." He grinned at her as he released her arm. "Might be kind of fun rounding you up again."

"Is that what you do with uncooperative women? Rope them and hog-tie them?"

"No, sweetheart." His glance was dangerously sexy. "I save that for the cooperative ones."

6

As soon as Tom arrived at the corral where a chestnut mare named Suzette pranced around, he asked Jose and Stan to bring Blaze, the scrub stallion, into the adjoining corral. A few of the hands and several of the guests had gathered on the far side of the corral, ready for the show. Tom had warned all the parents about the afternoon's event, in case they didn't want their kids to observe the breeding process, and he noticed none of the kids were around, either because they'd been kept away or because they didn't think mating horses were interesting enough to give up a swim for.

Cleo rested her arms on the top rail and propped her chin on her hands. Tom thought she looked really natural out here by the corral. Deidre never had, no matter how many weeks she'd spent on the ranch. Maybe it was Cleo's lack of heavy makeup, her unpolished nails and casual clothes. Or maybe it was the way she seemed to look at ranch life with an intensity of purpose, as if she wanted to understand how things worked around here. Deidre had never seemed to care.

Of course, Cleo had a purpose, and once that was satisfied, she might lose interest completely. He was impressed by Cleo's stubbornness when she got an idea. He didn't meet too many people he shared that trait with. Her stubbornness might cheat them both out of some really great sex, though, unless he used her special rule about mixing business with pleasure against her.

If he seduced her, he'd take himself out of the calendar project and end that debate once and for all. All he needed was the right set of circumstances, and she'd go up like a pile of dry kindling. A strand of golden hair blew across her cheek, and he resisted the impulse to comb it back for her. Now was not the time.

Blaze, an old palomino with too many conformation faults to be considered a good stud, came prancing into the corral next to Suzette's. Handling Blaze was a two-man job, so Stan and Jose each had a rope on the stallion.

"What's up with this?" Cleo asked. "He can't get to her."

"He's not supposed to. Blaze is the teaser."

Cleo turned to look at him. "Excuse me?"

He met her gaze. "We have to make sure Suzette's in heat before we bring in Chico, the stud. Otherwise she could bite him, or kick the devil out of him if she's not interested. I can't take a chance on that happening with Chico, who's worth a hell of a lot more than old Blaze."

"Oh." Cleo returned her attention to Suzette. "There've been a few times I could have used a set of hooves, myself."

Tom lowered his voice, although there was little danger of anyone overhearing. "Are you referring to recent history?"

She didn't look at him, but her throat moved in a swallow. "No. My attraction to you is real, and extremely inconvenient."

Or convenient, looking at the situation another way, he thought. "Just checking. I'd hate like hell to get kicked." He watched Suzette sidle over to the fence where Blaze strained at his ropes. Suzette lifted her tail and allowed Blaze a sniff. Good sign.

"I don't imagine you get kicked very often," Cleo murmured.

"Not if I can help it."

"He looks very eager," she said.

"Oh, he's eager, all right. Pretty soon it'll be very obvious how eager he is."

Blaze struggled against the ropes as he tried to lean over the fence, and his arousal became evident to anyone who cared to look between his hind legs.

"I...uh...see what you mean," Cleo muttered. "My goodness."

He gave her a sideways glance. "Males aren't built to keep secrets."

"What about her? How can you tell if she's in heat?"

"By the look in her eyes."

She turned her head and met his gaze.

He drew in a quick breath at the tumult in those blue depths. Oh, yes, she was ready. More than ready.

"Are we talking about horses?" she asked.

"You are." A high-pitched squeal from Suzette brought his attention back to the corral. Suzette humped her back in an awkward little bucking motion, laid her ears back and squealed again. "All right," Tom said. "We're in business." He raised his voice. "Jose, Stan—take him away and get Chico."

"Right, boss!" Jose said. He and Stan fought to pull the stallion away from the fence. Blaze fought back, whinnying and planting his haunches to brace himself against the tug of the ropes.

"That's terrible!" Cleo said. "Poor Blaze."

"That's business." Tom glanced at her. "Isn't that what you told me?"

She pushed away from the fence and faced him. "If you're implying that my photo sessions in any way resemble this...this..."

He kept his voice down. "I'm not implying. I'm saying it straight out. The whole time I watched you work with Jeeter, all I could think about was Blaze. I don't know if you have a boyfriend who gets the benefit of all those hormones flying around, but I refuse to be treated like some scrub stallion while another guy gets to take part in the main event."

Her lips were parted, her breath coming fast. Tom figured that if they weren't standing out in the wide-open spaces with eight or ten people as witnesses, now would be a fine time to touch a match to that dry kindling. From the corner of his eye he saw Chico, a magnificent dark bay, being brought into the corral with Suzette.

"I don't have a boyfriend," Cleo said, her gaze never leaving his face.

Damn, but that was good news. "Then you must get a little frustrated at times, darlin'." While he continued to keep his attention firmly on Cleo, he was also aware of the mare and stallion maneuvering through their courtship ritual—the sniffing, the little nips, the snorts and squeals. He remained alert to any signs of trouble, but all seemed to be going well.

"My frustrations aren't your concern," Cleo said.

"I could make them my concern."

"No." She licked her lips.

His groin tightened as he remembered how her tongue had felt inside his mouth and how hungry she'd been for his kiss. Instinct told him the horses would mate any moment now. "Hey, I don't want you to miss anything." He cupped her elbow and turned her to face the corral again just as Chico lunged over Suzette's hindquarters and buried himself in her. Tom felt the shudder go through Cleo.

He wondered if she might run from the blatant sexual message being spelled out in the corral, and this time he planned to let her go. He'd made his point. But she stayed through it all, trembling but focused.

Tom hated to leave her now. If he could walk her back to her cabin, they might settle things this afternoon. But he had duties connected with this breeding event. "I have to go," he murmured, squeezing her arm gently.

She nodded, not looking at him.

"If you need anything, you know where to find me."

She nodded again.

He walked away, wishing that just this once someone else could shoulder his responsibilities. He had no doubt that if he could take Cleo's hand and lead her to the nearest secluded place, she would make love with him until they were both exhausted. But an hour from now, the spell might be broken.

CLEO WASN'T SURE how she made it back to her cabin. Images of stallions and sexy cowboys swirled through her head as she stumbled away from the corral to find a measure of privacy so that she could think. She couldn't give in to this lust for Tom McBride, could she? Then she wouldn't be able to use him for the calendar, and she'd jeopardize her husband hunt in the bargain. But as she opened the door of her cabin and walked into the refreshing coolness, neither of those reasons seemed strong enough to deny herself the pleasure to be found in Tom's arms.

A courier packet lay on her bed—the contact sheets of her firefighters Bernie had shipped out yesterday. Relief flooded Cleo at the prospect of a familiar job. She knew from experience that choosing the photographs for a calendar didn't stir up the same cravings as the photo shoots themselves. The selection of prints required a dispassionate, critical eye, and one of the reasons she'd made it so far in her profession was her ability to coolly judge her own work.

Still standing beside the bed, she opened the packet and skimmed the note from Bernie, which contained nothing but routine information...until she came to the last paragraph.

Your father called. He's interested in using your *Montana Men* calendar as a premium for Sphinx customers this Christmas. I told him I'd check with you. Frankly, although the extra exposure would be nice—I think the company's planning TV and print ads—I'd love you to tell him to go jump in the lake. This calendar will sell big without his help. By the way, found a husband yet?

B.

Cleo sat on the bed and reread the paragraph. When her first calendar was scheduled, she'd asked her father if he'd consider using it as a giveaway for his cosmetics customers, which would have provided national and international exposure when she needed it most. Asking had been difficult for her. But listening to his refusal had been sheer hell.

Now that she had created her own fame, he was willing to link his company's name with hers. She wasn't sure what she would do yet, but one thing was certain—this calendar would be the best damn thing she'd ever done. And that meant getting Tom McBride on the cover. Getting Tom to pose wouldn't be easy, but then nothing worth doing ever was. Her father had taught her that.

Cleo avoided Tom for the rest of the day and didn't go to the main house for dinner. Snacking from Juanita's refrigerator was more Cleo's style, anyway. She longed for a soak in the hot tub, but she couldn't take a chance that Tom might wander down to see if she was there. She didn't trust herself around him with all her clothes on at the moment, let alone when she was lounging naked in bubbling mineral water.

Instead, she used her evening to choose twelve firefighters from the contact sheets Bernie had sent. The task absorbed all her attention, and when she'd finished, she discovered she was tired enough to go to bed. After she packaged up her choices and sealed them into a return envelope, she crawled under the covers. She'd better enjoy the innerspring mattress tonight, she told herself, because the following night she'd be camped under the stars. Tom would be there, but so would a lot of other people, not to mention dogs, horses and cattle. Cleo judged the situation safe enough to keep her from falling into temptation.

She slipped easily toward sleep, despite the same yipping, rustling and howling she'd experienced the night before. Maybe the mountain air and sunshine had worked some sort of magic during the day, because she felt incredibly relaxed and peaceful. Or maybe, she thought briefly before she drifted off, she was getting used to Montana.

WHEN MORNING ARRIVED, bringing with it the prospect of seeing Tom constantly for the next two days, her stomach jumped around as if she'd just finished riding the Coney Island roller coaster. She missed breakfast because she spent a ridiculous amount of time deciding what to wear and what to pack. Finally, she settled on jeans, a chambray shirt and her vest. She packed a change of underwear, a few personal toiletries and several candy bars, all of which fit into the pockets of her camera bag. She put on her sunglasses and grabbed a jacket on her way out the door.

The sun had baked the dew from the grass, leaving behind a scent so fresh it triggered memories of a summer when she was fourteen. Normally she'd spent her school vacations in a round of music and dance lessons. Her father had never taken time off, and so neither had she or her mother, but that year she'd been invited by a girlfriend to spend two glorious weeks at the family's summer home in Connecticut. To Cleo, both then and now, the sun-warmed grass smelled of freedom.

She could see riders gathering beside the corral where mounts in the process of being saddled were lined up along the hitching post. The black-and-white dog she'd noticed the first day, whose name was Trixie, was trotting around the group in obvious anticipation of a trip. Nearby, a team of horses had been hitched to a wagon loaded with supplies.

Even from this distance, Cleo picked Tom out of the

crowd. She recognized his walk, the set of his shoulders and the way he wore his hat. Forty-eight hours ago they'd been strangers, and already he'd become alarmingly familiar to her. Well, that was good, she decided, adjusting the strap of her camera bag on her shoulder as she started toward the corral. The more familiar he was, the better she'd photograph him when the time came.

As she approached, she recognized Jeeter and Jose, as well. That was lucky, she thought. Jose was a definite calendar possibility, and this would give her a chance to see if he was interested. She might even be able to set up a shoot while they were on the trail. *He's also a husband prospect*, she reminded herself. With that in mind, she tried to focus exclusively on Jose as he led another horse out of the corral, but her attention kept wandering in Tom's direction.

The scents and sounds of the corral brought back thoughts of yesterday, standing beside Tom while a stallion had his way with a willing mare. That man had known exactly what he was doing, piling that event on top of their encounter in the barn. If she succumbed to his considerable charms, she wouldn't get her cover photo. No matter how arousing the circumstances, she needed to remember that.

Luckily, for the next two days at least, she'd have chaperons. She glanced over the five guests who'd volunteered to help move the cattle. She remembered them vaguely from her first meal at the ranch and chance encounters during the day and a half she'd been at the Whispering Winds, but she'd zoned out on their names.

The young couple that looked fresh out of college had been married about a year and lived in Massachusetts. The second couple had a fourteen-year-old daughter, and Tom helped the girl adjust her stirrups while both her parents stood by and offered advice in a clipped Boston accent.

At one point, Tom turned his back to the parents, glanced up at the girl and winked.

She gave him a smile back, and Cleo figured Tom had just made a friend for life. No teenager appreciated that kind of parental hovering.

"That should do it, Laura." Tom positioned the girl's booted foot in the stirrup. "Stand up on the balls of your feet and let me check."

"I still think they should be shorter," her mother said.

Laura stood in the stirrups and got an approving nod from Tom. "Western riding is different from English, Mom," Laura said.

"Well, I want mine shorter than that."

Tom turned around to speak to her and noticed Cleo for the first time. An expression of welcome lit his face before he swung his attention to Laura's mother. "We'll adjust them any way you like, Mrs. Preston." He glanced down the row of horses. "Jose? Can you get the Prestons mounted up? And bring out Dynamite for Ms. Griffin?"

Dynamite? Cleo gulped.

"Sure thing, boss."

Cleo couldn't suppress feeling a flicker of desire as Tom walked over to her. He was one fine-looking cowboy.

He nudged his hat back with his thumb and smiled.

"So you're going."

"I said I would. But about this horse you're putting me on. I—"

"I admire a woman of her word." His gaze traveled over her. "You need a hat."

"I don't have one. I'll be fine. Listen, is Dynamite a very—"

"Everybody in my outfit wears a hat." He took her arm. "Come on. Let's see what we can find."

"I don't like hats." She went along with him because it was less embarrassing than digging in her heels and creating a scene. "I never wear them."

"You will on this ride. I won't have you keeling over from sunstroke or burning that pretty little nose of yours."

"I have sunscreen. And lots of hair to protect me from sunstroke. And my nose isn't little."

He laughed as he towed her up the steps of the ranch house. "You're right. You've got one of those highborn sort of noses, but you won't look quite so regal if it's red as a bandanna."

"Oh, for heaven's sake. I feel like a little kid being told to wear her rubbers. I'm a big girl. I can take care of myself."

"In New York, maybe." Tom nodded to Luann, who was cleaning the ashes from the fireplace. "'Mornin', Luann."

"'Morning, Tom." She sat back on her heels and grinned at Cleo. "I'll bet he's getting you a hat."

"So he says."

Tom pulled her into his office and flipped the door closed. "You do need something to cover your head, but first I need this." He took off his hat and his mouth came down on hers.

They picked right up where they'd left off, and the barriers she'd worked so hard to construct, the reasons that she shouldn't allow this, crumpled before the on-slaught of his lips. She should be pushing him away instead of reveling in the morning-coffee taste of him, breathing in the scent of his aftershave and the ever-present combination of leather and aroused male. God, he could kiss.

He held her tight against him and lifted his head to gaze down at her. "'Mornin', Cleo."

She tried to catch her breath. "You're trying to cause me trouble, aren't you, cowboy?"

"I'm trying to ease your troubles, lady. You've been dodging me since yesterday, haven't you?"

"I had work to do."

His hands slid down her back and cupped her bottom. "So did I, but I could have slipped you into my schedule."

She was turning into a molten mass of need, but she tried not to let him know how much he affected her. She took a deep breath. "I'm holding out for my cover photo, Tom."

His mouth curved in a slow, sensuous smile. "Damn, but you're a stubborn female."

And you're about the sexiest man I've ever met. Cleo looked into his mesmerizing gray eyes and gave thanks that Luann was just outside the door and seven people were waiting for them at the corral. Without those considerations, he might have been able to talk her into almost anything right now, including a session on top of his massive oak desk.

"We need to get going," she said.

"That's what I've been trying to tell you, woman. Life's too short."

"Back to the corral."

"Oh. Them."

"And after all this fuss I'd better show up with a hat."

"I was dead serious about the hat." He released her and walked over to a row of pegs where hats of various sizes and colors hung. "I was dead serious about the rest of it, too, but I intend to get your head covered first." He picked out a cream-colored Stetson and walked back to her. "Let's see how this suits you."

She held out her hand. "I'll put it on after we mount up."

"Nope. We'll make sure it fits right now, so I don't hear any excuses out on the trail as to why you're not wearing it. Hold still."

"Honestly." But with him that close, she had to hold still or risk throwing herself into his arms again.

He settled the hat on her head and tugged the brim down in front. Then he stood back, thumbs hooked in his belt loops, to survey the result. Slowly a grin creased his face.

"What?" She looked around for a mirror, but found none. "I look ridiculous, right?"

"Nope. You look like you were made to wear that hat. Keep it."

"Now that's *really* ridiculous. Once I leave here, I'll have no use for it." Once she left here, she wouldn't see Tom McBride again, either. The thought created such an empty feeling that she pushed it aside. "Because you're making such a big deal about this hat thing, I'll wear it for the cattle drive, but after that I'm returning it."

"I wouldn't be too hasty about that. The right hat is a rare discovery. Some people try on a hundred before they find the one that fits their head and personality.

That one's perfect for you." He picked up his own from the desk and put it on. "Let's go." He strode over to the door and opened it.

Fascinated by his assessment, she hurried after him. "Why is it so perfect?"

He kept walking. "Frames your face real nice without dominating it. A face like yours doesn't need a lot of geegaws to distract people. The color's good against your blond hair. The crown's about right. Wouldn't want one too short, with those long legs of yours." He glanced at her as they crossed the ranch yard and headed toward the corrals. "It's classy, but that little feather in the hatband gives it spirit. Like I said, it's a great fit."

A warm glow settled over her as she absorbed his evaluation. His matter-of-fact delivery gave the elaborate compliment even more impact. If this was a line he was feeding her just to get what he wanted, he was very skilled at it—she was swallowing every single word without a single twinge of big-city cynicism.

By the time they arrived at the corrals, she'd decided that she positively loved the hat.

7

"PICK UP THE PACE, Dynamite. We're lagging behind again, horse." Finishing off her candy bar, Cleo nudged the buckskin mare in the ribs and clucked encouragingly. The truth was, their pokiness was as much her fault as Dynamite's. Riding up through a wildflower-strewn ravine—what Tom informed everyone was called a coulee out in these parts—Cleo lifted her gaze to snow-draped mountains that commanded a huge chunk of cobalt sky. Turning in her saddle, she watched the ranch transform into a child's diorama complete with a meandering stream that flashed silver in the sun.

The trail wound through a stand of aspens, their heart-shaped leaves quivering in the breeze. Beyond the aspen grove lay a meadow where a young buck lifted his antlered head, sniffed the air and bolted, his white tail lifting like a flag as he disappeared into the feathery protection of pine and spruce. Birds chattered and swooped through the trees, daubing color against the deep green of the forest, and the tangy scent of evergreens spiced the air.

Camera at the ready, Cleo was in no hurry to cover ground. She'd let everyone else go ahead of her while she used up one roll and started on another.

As for Dynamite, the mare was definitely in no hurry. Someone with a sense of humor had named this horse,

Cleo decided as she dug her heels in again and clucked. She was following Jeeter, who drove the wagon, and Tom, who rode alongside. Much as she enjoyed the leisurely pace and the chance to take some shots of the unbelievable scenery, she didn't want to lose sight of the group. Not when there could be cougars around.

"Move it, baby," Cleo said, getting more aggressive with her heels. "Bringing up the rear is one thing, but we're not even doing a credible job of that."

Dynamite's ears flicked back and her plodding stride accelerated slightly, but not much.

Ahead of them, Tom stopped talking with Jeeter and glanced over his shoulder. Then he wheeled his big chestnut and loped back toward Cleo. He looked mighty fine mounted on that flame-colored animal, Cleo thought, admiring how his body moved in rhythm with the gelding's stride. She'd never noticed before how much the rocking motion of a rider's hips mimicked the sexual act.

As he reached her and turned his mount to keep pace with Dynamite, all sorts of suggestive behavior leaped to Cleo's mind. The wagon had disappeared over a rise, leaving them in a tantalizingly private setting. But she must not allow herself to be tantalized.

"I can't seem to find the fuse on this horse of yours, McBride," she said.

He grinned. "I didn't know you wanted a Derby contender." He reined in his prancing horse. "Easy, Red."

"I didn't want a horse like yours, that's for sure. But with this mare, sweet as she is, I feel as if I may have to get out and push."

"I had the idea you hadn't ridden much recently, so I

was thinking of your backside." He paused, glanced at her and laughed. "Let me rephrase that."

"Oh, I'll bet that's exactly what you were thinking of, cowboy."

His gray eyes twinkled. "Okay, it probably was. It's a damn good-looking backside, and I'd hate to see it damaged."

Not a good topic, Cleo thought as her body responded to the intimate discussion. "I think I could manage a little more speed without a problem. And what about when we find the cattle? Can she keep up?"

"She'll be fine. In her prime she was a good little cow pony, but she's semiretired now. I wanted you on a steady horse, and she's the steadiest one we have on the ranch. She won't spook and she'll stick by you if you happen to fall off."

Cleo was touched that he seemed to care so much about her welfare. "And what joker named this mare Dynamite?"

"I did."

"With tongue in cheek, right?"

"Nope." Tom kept his restless horse under a tight rein. "A kid doesn't joke around when he's naming his horse."

"She was your horse when you were a kid?" Cleo leaned down to examine Dynamite's muzzle for gray hairs and noticed quite a few. "Just how old is she?"

"Twenty-six."

"Yikes! Now I feel guilty for making her go faster. Shouldn't she be turned out to pasture or something?"

"Not when she's sound, and likes to get out and see a bit of the world, right, Dynamite?"

The mare's ears swiveled back at the mention of her name.

"I watched her being born," Tom continued. "When my dad gave her to me, he might as well have given me the world on a silver platter, I was so excited. She was a fast little pony and had the habit of exploding into a run, so I named her Dynamite. She has great-great-grandchildren on the ranch."

"Wow." Cleo had new respect for the mare, and a feeling of tenderness for the cowboy who was letting her ride his first horse. "All I ever had when I was a kid was a hamster."

"Never could figure that, keeping rodents as pets. Around here we have cats to get rid of the damn things."

"Ah, but you never knew Squeaky. He was an exceptional rodent. I taught him tricks." He'd been the only livestock on her Lincoln Log ranch, so she'd made do.

Tom chuckled. "I'll bet you did." He glanced at her. "I can just picture this little towhead training her hamster."

"He was good company." Cleo smiled at the memory of the furry little creature she hadn't thought about in years. She'd been devastated when he died.

"You don't have brothers or sisters?" Tom asked.

"Nope. It's up to me to carry the family banner."

"Sounds like a heavy one."

Cleo shrugged. "You're carrying your family banner, too, now that your sister isn't involved in the ranch."

"Yeah." He shook his head. "And I didn't know the true financial picture until a couple of years ago, when Dad finally had to turn everything over to me."

"Not good?"

"Not great. I—" He paused and looked at her in surprise. "How in hell did we get off on that?"

"It's weighing on your mind, isn't it?"

He stared off into the shadowy depths of the trees on either side of the trail. "Nah," he said, and gave her a cocky grin. "Not really."

She didn't believe him, but he was apparently too proud to reveal the true extent of his worry. "Pose for me," she said. "As Jeeter mentioned, it's a painless way to pick up some extra cash, and it might lead to other monetary gain. It might even increase your business."

"Which would mean enlarging the ranch, and I like the size it is now."

She did, too. She couldn't picture the Whispering Winds as a giant operation. "Okay, then forget that. Just think about your fee. I told you I'd negotiate a higher one for you, because I really want you on the calendar."

He gazed at her. "I'd settle for having you really want me, period."

Oh, she did. She certainly did. And they'd been alone way too long. She cleared the huskiness from her voice. "I think we'd better catch up to the others."

"Scared of me, Cleo?"

"Let's just say that your goal runs counter to mine."

"And you're afraid I might be able to talk you out of that cover picture and into my bed, aren't you?"

Her nerves tightened and hummed, ready for action. "The talking isn't what worries me."

His tone was low and easy on her ears. "I'll never take you where you don't want to go."

"Then I think you'd better take me back to the others. Now."

He sighed. "Probably so." As they passed a small

pine, he reached up, broke off a branch and held it out toward her. "Whack Dynamite a few times on the rump with this and she'll go for you."

Cleo shrank back from the offered stick. "Hit a great-great-grandmother? I couldn't!"

"Somebody's got to. I have a powerful urge to pull you off that horse and make love to you on a bed of pine needles this very minute."

She looked into his eyes, heavy with need, and her pulse raced at the picture he'd created in her mind.

"Hang on, Cleo."

She grasped the saddle horn just in time. The switch came down on Dynamite's rump at the same moment Tom whooped a command, and the little mare sprang straight out of her walk into a gallop. Cleo lost her stirrups but managed to regain them as the trees flashed by on either side of her. Pounding hooves behind her told her that Tom was following, making sure she was okay.

The speed felt good, once she was used to it. The forward momentum and whipping wind helped take her mind off her sexual frustration. But she couldn't ride like this for the entire time she was in Montana, and when she stopped, she'd want Tom all over again. She needed to create more distractions for herself, somehow, perhaps, by focusing on Jose and planning how she would pose him for the calendar, at least during this cattle drive.

WATCHING HER was sweet torture, Tom thought. She'd proved to be surprisingly good with the hazing of the cattle once they located the herd. When Dynamite demonstrated her cow-pony moves, Cleo managed to stay aboard and even work in a candy-bar break. Tom was so busy keeping a protective eye on Cleo, he ended up having to chase down a cow that slipped by him, much to Jose's amusement.

Jose happened to end up beside Tom while they were crossing a shallow stream. Next to them the cows flowed in a rust-brown river, the sound of their hooves splashing in a steady rhythm punctuated with irritated-sounding moos. "You like her, don't you, boss?" Jose asked.

Tom didn't bother to deny it. "I suppose I'm making a damn fool of myself, too."

"Not really," Jose said, loyal to the last. "It'd be easy to do, though, with a woman who looks like her." He guided his horse onto dry ground.

Tom followed and came alongside Jose again. He had a few questions for the cowboy. "Has she asked you to pose for the calendar yet?"

"Yep." Jose slapped his rope against his thigh as a cow tried to veer out of formation. "Hiya!" he shouted, heading the cow back into line.

"Gonna do it?" Tom felt a moment of unease, remembering the outrageous way Cleo had flirted with Jeeter.

"Guess so."

"Better talk to Jeeter and get a handle on how she works."

"I already did." Jose flicked a glance at his boss. "Jeeter says she comes on to the guy so she can get the right kind of picture. It's show business."

Tom's laugh was short. "That's one way of putting it."

"In your place, I wouldn't like the way she does things, either. But a dollar's a dollar, and Jeeter said you gave us the green light."

Tom pulled his hat lower over his eyes. "Hell, I can't stand in the way of your budding film career. I could be riding with the next Antonio Banderas, for all I know."

Jose laughed and shook his head. "I'm not counting on being a movie star, but I wouldn't mind the fee she's paying for the calendar. I could use a new saddle, and I've got my eye on a real beauty, silver-trimmed. I reckon I can flex my muscles for that." He grinned at Tom. "Not that you don't pay good, but I can't buy the rig I want on my wages from the Whispering Winds, boss."

"The way Cleo tells it, you make a pinup boy of yourself and your financial worries will be over. You'll head for Hollywood and that'll be the last I ever see of you."

"I couldn't leave this place," Jose said. "I've been working here ever since I turned sixteen."

"Which means you're in a rut, cowboy." In a way, Tom was relieved that a couple of his hands were getting this photo opportunity. Every time he looked at the ranch's debts, they cast a shadow bigger than the Madison Range they were riding into today. He was operating on such a small margin that if beef prices took a dive at market time, he'd go under, and so would the jobs of the people who were like family to him. Cleo might be unknowingly providing a cushion for Jose and Jeeter, at least.

"Jeeter says she asked you to pose, but you said no," Jose ventured.

"Jeeter's sure been flapping his jaws a lot. Guess I have to double up on that boy's duties, seeing as how he's got time to stand around and gossip." Tom headed off a calf who started to stray from the herd.

"Aw, Jeeter didn't mean any harm. He's just a kid,

with stars in his eyes because he thinks he's going to be famous, and he thinks everyone else wants to be famous, too."

"But you don't."

"Nope. I know exactly what I want out of this."

Tom looked at him and wished the guy could be a little uglier. The idea of Cleo getting cozy with him was damn unsettling.

Jose returned the look. "Don't worry, boss. All I'm after is a saddle."

MOVING THE HERD took the rest of the afternoon. Cleo enjoyed every minute of the constant activity, which reminded her a lot of Manhattan at rush hour. But eventually the cattle were transferred to their new pasture and the riders recrossed the stream and started back down the mountain. About an hour later, as the sun dipped behind the Madisons, Tom announced it was time to set up camp.

Cleo didn't realize how saddle-sore she was until she dismounted, but nobody else was complaining, so she kept her mouth shut. Laura and her parents obviously rode all the time in Massachusetts, and the young couple had been at the ranch a week, so they were already toughened up. Cleo shuddered to think what shape she'd have been in if Tom hadn't given her the horseback equivalent of a BarcaLounger.

They were camped in an open meadow bisected by a bubbling brook, a truly picturesque spot, if Cleo could just forget that bears and cougars roamed free in this country, and that she'd be sleeping in a bedroll with not so much as a canvas tent between her and the great outdoors. Dynamite seemed unconcerned as Cleo turned her out to graze on the lush grass, so Cleo decided to try for the same nonchalance.

While Tom unhitched the team of horses from the wagon and led them out to join the others in the meadow, everyone else gathered around the fire Jose had built. He had a kerosene cookstove going with what smelled like beef stew in a large kettle. Cleo hoped that cougars didn't have a special fondness for stew, because the aroma seemed to fill the meadow, and night was coming on fast. She'd been counting on Trixie as an early-warning system, but the dog was flopped by the fire, apparently asleep.

She'd pulled on her jacket against the chill, but the darkness that began to surround them made her shiver more than the cool night air. She'd never seen anything so black as the edge of the forest. Fingers of mist curled over the meadow, further obscuring Cleo's view.

"Did anybody bring a flashlight?" she asked the group in general.

Jeeter looked up from where he was unloading camp stools from the back of the wagon. "We have a few. Want one?"

"Uh, not just at the moment. I just wondered if we...had some."

"I think the firelight is much more romantic," said Amy, cuddling next to her young husband, Nick.

Cleo would have been happy with a bank of floodlights, say about the wattage of those used to illuminate Yankee Stadium.

"Yeah, this place is cool," Laura said. "It's exactly the sort of deserted spot aliens would pick to land."

"You've been watching too many movies," her father said. "Anything to drink in that wagon, Jeeter?"

"Sure. Everybody have a seat, and I'll take orders."

Cleo eyed the camp stools arranged around the fire circle, then pictured herself inching down to sit on one and the grimace of pain that would give away her delicate condition. She elected to stand. Jeeter got around to her drink order just as Tom came back from seeing to the horses. When Tom materialized out of the darkness looking so solid and safe, she had the urge to run into the protection of his arms. She'd actually moved a few steps in his direction before she caught herself and stopped.

"What'll you have, Cleo?" Jeeter asked.

Still watching Tom as he came toward her, she spoke without thinking, giving the response she would have in New York. "Perrier with a twist."

Tom grinned as he joined them. "Make sure you serve that in the Baccarat crystal while you're at it, Jeeter. You know where we keep it, don't you?"

"No, boss, I sure don't." Jeeter sounded totally mystified. "Isn't that some kind of board game?"

Cleo winced. Then she turned to Jeeter. "What do you have to drink, Jeeter?"

"Beer and soda pop, ma'am."

"Then I'll take a beer, Jeeter. Thanks."

"Boss? Want something?"

"Sure." Tom shoved back his hat. "I'll take a beer."

Cleo turned to him after Jeeter left. "A cowboy who knows his crystal. You're a fascinating combination, Tom."

"Not fascinating enough, apparently."

"I'm the only daughter of a business tycoon. I have personal discipline like you wouldn't believe."

"A tycoon, huh? And all you got was a hamster?"

"We lived in an elegant apartment in the city."

Tom nodded. "I know the kind." He paused as Jeeter brought them each a beer. He tipped his can against hers. "Here's looking at you, kid."

"*Casablanca*. Don't tell me you're a fan of old movies, too."

"Okay, I won't tell you that."

As she took a sip from her beer can, she conjured an image of curling up with him on the deep cushions of his couch to watch Humphrey Bogart and Ingrid Bergman, while a fire blazed on the hearth and snow whirled outside the windows. They'd have popcorn and beer, and after the movie they'd... No, they wouldn't, because by the time the winter snow arrived, she'd be long gone.

"How come you're not sitting over with the others on the camp stools?" he asked.

"Standing's nice."

"Uh-huh. You got a little sore, after all, didn't you?"

"Maybe."

"We always bring along some sports cream for that problem. I'll get you a tube and you can go off a ways from the group and rub some on." He set his beer on a nearby rock and turned toward the wagon.

"Wait. What do you mean, go off a ways from the group?"

He glanced back at her. "I figured you wouldn't want to be pulling down your jeans in front of everybody."

"But it's dark out there." As if to make her point, something howled off in the distance.

"Then take somebody with you. One of the other women."

"Oh, sure. The blind leading the blind. Amy's in a romantic haze and Laura's looking for aliens. And I don't want to give Laura's mother the satisfaction of knowing I'm sore. When she wasn't correcting Laura's riding form, she was correcting mine."

He smiled. "Want me to go with you?"

"That's even more dangerous. I'll just put up with it."

"No, you won't. Hell, I'll send Jeeter out there with you, and have him take a rifle if it'll make you feel safer. He'll turn his back."

"Tom, please. I'd be embarrassed for Jeeter to know. Let's just keep this our little secret, okay?"

He shook his head. "You have to ride back to the ranch tomorrow, and you'll be so stiff you won't get your calendar work done. I've seen how much you move around when you're shooting. Here's the deal. I'll go with you. I'll take a rifle. Believe me, I'm not going to try anything funny with guests no more than thirty yards away."

"Oh, all right." Cleo decided she was becoming paranoid about the temptations he afforded. Of course they wouldn't get involved in hanky-panky when other people were so near. And she didn't want to be in worse shape tomorrow because she'd refused the treatment offered. She set her beer next to his on the rock.

Tom left and returned a few minutes later with a tube of ointment, a flashlight and a rifle. He handed her the ointment. "Let's go."

"After you."

He cradled the rifle under one arm, flicked on the flashlight and swung the beam back and forth across the grass as they walked into the darkness.

Cleo followed right on his heels. "Shouldn't you be

shining that thing higher up, so it reflects off the eyes of the bear, or whatever comes along to eat us?"

He chuckled. "I'll hear something that big. I'm checking for snakes."

"That's it. I'm leaving." She whirled and started back.

He caught her by a finger through her belt loop and pulled her back. "Come on. Don't be a such a greenhorn."

She turned to face him. "I *am* a greenhorn. And proud of it."

He turned off the flashlight and tucked it in his pocket.

"Turn that thing on."

"In a minute." He nudged her hat back on her head and cupped her face in his free hand. "Kiss me, Cleo. It's gonna be a long night."

She wanted his kiss, no matter how much she tried to deny it. "I knew following you out here was a bad—"

His mouth came down on hers, ending her protest and playing hell with her self-control. There was nothing leisurely about his kiss. He ravaged her mouth, took possession with his tongue and left her pounding with desire. Then he pulled away, tugged her hat in place and reached in his pocket for the flashlight.

She could barely breathe.

"I thought you could use something else to think about besides critters," he said, switching on the flashlight and sweeping it around the area where they stood.

If that had been his strategy, it had worked really well, she thought. Two powerful emotions couldn't co-exist within her, apparently, and lust had just obliterated fear.

He gestured with the beam of the flashlight. "Over there's as good a spot as any. I'll keep the light below your knees. Just walk about ten paces away and pull down your pants."

She took a shaky breath and followed his instructions. "I'll bet you say that to all the girls."

"Only the girls who look good in that hat."

"And how many has that been?"

"One."

8

TOM PULLED the last shift of guard duty, taking the few hours just before dawn. Jose, Jeeter and Tom had divided the night into thirds, as they always did when they had either people or animals to watch over. They didn't make a big deal of it, not wanting to alarm the dudes, but they couldn't afford to have a grizzly sneak up on the campsite. Tom had noticed that Cleo had looked immensely relieved when she'd discovered that someone would be patrolling the area all through the night.

He'd teased her about being a greenhorn, but he'd rather have the guests show her sort of caution than think they were in Disneyland and the animals could all talk and sing songs. Being out in the wilderness of Montana meant accepting some level of risk, but not everyone was willing to face that. Therefore, he took the responsibility for them and made sure someone stayed on guard, someone who could handle a rifle and keep a cool head.

It had been a quiet night. With the fire reduced to embers and the stars bright as the New York skyline after dark, visibility was pretty good. Jose had reported seeing a black bear venture partway out of the trees before heading back in. Tom had watched for the bear to reappear, but it hadn't. Bears weren't usually a problem unless they'd learned to raid campsites and had a taste for human junk food. Then they could be deadly in their search for the goodies they craved.

Tom was seeing more of that happening in his beloved wilderness, and he hated it, just as he hated the disappearance of the elegant cougars. He needed to keep his herd intact, but if at all possible, he'd do it without killing one of the giant cats.

As the stars lost some of their brilliance and the edge of the horizon began to lighten, he meandered over to the side of camp where Cleo slept. He took satisfaction in knowing that she slept, even though she'd stirred restlessly when the wolves had started in about an hour ago. Tom had always thought they sounded mournful instead of frightening. Wolves were another sore point with Montana ranchers now that the environmental faction had reintroduced them, but Tom figured they were part of the mix, just like cougars. Montana wouldn't be the same without predators.

The wolves had quieted, and Cleo looked peaceful now, her hand curled under her chin, her golden hair spilling over the rolled-up jacket she'd made into a pillow. She couldn't know that he'd sacrifice himself before letting anything happen to her. He wasn't sure exactly when it had clicked in, but he'd developed a protective feeling about her that probably spelled trouble. The minute he felt this urge to take care of a woman, it usually meant that he'd let down his guard and eventually she'd play him for a fool. Deidre sure as hell had.

He watched Cleo sleep and tried to pinpoint when he'd felt that telltale tug at his heart. Maybe when he'd seen how much like a cowgirl she looked in that hat, or when he'd noticed she was lagging behind and trying valiantly to coax Dynamite into a trot. Maybe it was the picture she'd painted of teaching her hamster tricks, or the plucky way she'd helped drive the cattle and then kept quiet about how sore she was.

In any case, more than lust drew him now, which could be dangerous. He could forget the lure of a woman's body, but once she'd started working on his mind, he'd remember her for the rest of his life.

From the corner of his eye, across the meadow, he caught a movement. Turning slowly, he glimpsed a huge bull moose coming out of the trees, headed for the brook. The moose was only an indistinct shadow now, his rack of antlers rising like an unattainable, perfect trophy in a hunter's dream. Tom never had developed a taste for hunting. He killed only when there was no choice—if an animal was a threat or very sick. He wouldn't lead guests on hunting trips, either, although many of his neighbors brought in extra money that way.

Moving carefully so as not to startle the moose, Tom crouched and gently shook Cleo's shoulder.

She opened her eyes at once, making him wonder if she'd been as fast asleep as he'd thought.

He leaned close to her ear and pushed the silky hair aside so he could whisper to her. Breathing in the flowery scent of her skin, he wanted to linger, to nibble and enjoy, but he knew she'd want this wildlife shot to take home to New York. "There's a bull moose approaching the stream," he murmured. "Move slowly and get your camera. It should be light enough soon for you to get a great picture of him."

She nodded and began crawling carefully out of her bedroll. He stood and kept an eye on the moose, and in

no time Cleo stood beside him, shivering slightly, her
camera hanging around her neck. He leaned down to
her bedroll, shook out her bundled jacket and eased it
over her arms.

She smiled her gratitude, and his heart turned over.

She was a beauty in the morning. He took note of the
breeze that lifted a lock of her hair. The wind was
blowing toward them, which meant they might be able
to sneak closer without being scented.

He mouthed *follow me*, and she nodded again. Watching each step to make sure he didn't step on a twig and
shatter the morning silence, he crept forward. Looking
like a ghost stepping slowly through the ground fog,
the moose reached the rushing water and gazed
around. Tom froze. As the moose lowered his head to
drink, Tom started soundlessly forward again.

The moose lifted his head, water dripping from his
muzzle, and Tom paused, knowing they dared go no
closer or the animal would vanish back into the forest.
Cleo put her hand on Tom's shoulder and squeezed, as
if to signal to him that this was the spot. As they stood
rigidly waiting, the first light of morning tipped the
bull's mighty antlers with bronze.

Click. The sound of the camera's shutter was no
louder than a cricket's chirp, but the moose swiveled
his massive head and stared straight at them, as if he'd
known of their presence all along. *Click.* The shutter
opened and closed a second time. The moose turned
and walked regally away, with no apparent haste, until
he was lost in the shadows of the trees.

"Do you think you got it?" Tom asked, speaking
softly as he watched the trees where the moose had disappeared.

"I got it." Her voice was rich with joy. "Oh, Tom, wasn't he magnificent?"

"Yeah." He turned toward her. "You asked me to show you what makes this place so special to me. I think I just did."

"Do you see stuff like that all the time?"

"Not all the time, but often enough to make all the hassles worthwhile."

"Thank you for waking me up."

"You're welcome." He couldn't help himself from touching her cheek. "How do you feel?"

"On the outside? A little stiff. On the inside? Like a kid at Christmas."

He smiled. "Welcome to the life of a cowpuncher. Most of the time you're stiff and sore from the work, but you have the most beautiful office in the world."

"No kidding." She gazed up at the mountains as sunlight gilded the snowy peaks. "I had no idea, Tom."

Easy, he cautioned himself. She might be falling in love with Montana. Lots of folks did that. It didn't mean much, in the long run. They went home, got back in their comfortable routine and forgot the wonder of a mountain morning like this one. Still, he'd never heard that awestruck tone in Deidre's voice. She'd liked the idea of being married to a Montana rancher because it sounded exotic to her New York friends. She hadn't liked the reality all that much.

"I have a very personal question to ask," Cleo said.

"Okay."

"You can tell me to mind my own business."

"Okay."

"Why...why did you get divorced?" She looked up at

him and quickly glanced away. "Sorry. I shouldn't have asked."

That she had her mind on a question so close to his own thoughts shook him. "Why did you ask?"

"I don't know. It's just that you don't seem like the divorcing kind, and I can't believe a woman would give up...all this."

"I don't think it was so tough to give up. Deidre had her priorities. Being married to me wasn't one of them."

Something unreadable was going on behind those blue eyes of hers. "I guess you take the whole idea of marriage pretty seriously," she said.

"If you don't take it seriously, what's the point in getting married?"

She looked uncomfortable. "Well, of course, a person should take it seriously, to a point. But as for having a marriage control your whole life, I think that—"

"It damn well should control your whole life. It controlled mine, so why shouldn't it have controlled hers? I was standing here thinking that you weren't anything like her, but maybe I was wrong. Maybe you would have sided with her. Career comes first, and a husband is just a handy convenience."

She flushed. "Career has always come first for men, though, hasn't it? What did you do, expect her to give up modeling?"

"Just for a while." He tried to stem the tide of anger rising in him. "She could have gone back to it."

"Not likely!" Her eyes flashed blue fire. "That's not the kind of job where you take a leave of absence to play house. You miss a step and you're history. I don't suppose you ever considered giving up ranching, now, did you? The little woman has to make the adjustments, while the man—"

"The *man* finds out too late that the little *woman* aborted their baby! Since when did you get the idea that men have all the control? A woman has the ultimate control!"

She looked stricken. "Oh, Tom. Tom, I'm sorry. I didn't realize."

He stared down at the ground, where dew sparkled like tears on the grass. "Nothing to be done about it now. Shouldn't have said anything." He was shaking, dammit. Worse yet, he could hear people stirring at the campsite. He'd probably woken them up with his shouting. Wonderful.

Cleo touched his arm. "Tom..."

"I need to check on the horses."

"I'll go with you."

"No." He gazed at her with regret. "It's probably just as well we got this argument out of the way. You'd think after going a few rounds with one New York woman I'd have sense enough to stay away from the next one who came along. Guess I'm a slow learner."

"Tom, I'm not..." She looked confused and didn't finish the sentence.

"I'm not saying you'd be sneaky, like Deidre. But you think like her. You've got a foothold on that success ladder, and you're not about to let some guy loosen that hold. You have a right to think like that. And I have a right to stay the hell away from you before I get myself in trouble again." He turned and headed out into the meadow where the horses grazed on the dew-soaked grass.

Thank God for this land, he thought as he took a

deep, calming breath. The women might come and go, but the land never disappointed him.

THE CATTLE DRIVE seemed to have acted like a fountain of youth for Dynamite. Either that or the little mare was eager to get back to her corral, Cleo thought. Head up and steps light, Dynamite pranced near the head of the group heading down the mountain. That was fine with Cleo. She'd lost her taste for picture-taking.

Tom was absolutely right about her, she thought as she rode along in the crisp air of a high-country morning. Career was her top priority, as it always had been for her father. Her mother had been a handy convenience. Growing up with that role model, Cleo had seen the advantages for the dominant person in the marriage, and she'd made up her mind to be that dominant person.

There was nothing wrong with her plan, she thought belligerently. Men had been working the system that way for years, so why shouldn't she turn the tables, find a docile man to play the supportive role, and get on with becoming famous? For the next few days all she needed to do was concentrate on her calendar and her husband-hunting. Not every cowboy in this valley thought like Tom. And if they didn't appeal to her quite as much as he did, well, that was the sacrifice she'd have to make. He wasn't the man for her.

Unfortunately, she wasn't making any progress getting Tom to pose for her calendar cover, either. In fact, after their blowup in the meadow, she doubted he'd want anything more to do with her, whether she had a camera in her hand or not. Well, good. She needed to forget him and get on with her work. Maybe Jose would make a good cover.

The sound of a trotting horse alerted her to someone coming from behind. Wondering if it could be Tom wanting to smooth things over, she turned expectantly and discovered Laura drawing alongside.

Pleasure glowed on Laura's fourteen-year-old face. "I ditched the mom and dad units. I found a wide place on the trail and rode around the wagon, but then the trail narrowed again and they're stuck behind it."

Cleo couldn't help laughing. It was so like the sort of thing she would have done at that age. "Parents can be a trial sometimes."

"Really. They treat me like a kid."

Cleo made sure she didn't smile at that. Fourteen was a very tough age, as she well remembered.

"I'm buying one of your calendars when I get home," Laura said. "I think what you do is so cool."

"Thanks."

"I can hardly wait until I can get a job. And my own apartment." Her young jaw firmed. "And I'm going to college where I want to, and not where they want me to."

Cleo understood that tone of rebellion well. She'd used it herself enough times. "It's tough when they try to control your every move."

"Did your parents do that?"

"Oh, you bet. I'm an only daughter, too, and I know the pressures you're under. Your parents remind me of mine, always after me to be perfect."

"I know! I hate that!"

"Well, you're their only shot, Laura. They get to concentrate all their hopes on you. Part of the time I loved being the center of attention, but most of the time I wanted a brother or sister, just to take the heat off me."

Laura giggled. "I used to beg them to adopt a kid. I went into this whole routine about the poor children in the ghetto. But they never went for the idea. I think they count how many times I breathe each day."

"I used to think that, too. I used to think I couldn't sneeze without them knowing about it, and telling me how I could sneeze better next time."

"Yeah." Laura grinned. "Anyway, I'll bet your parents don't control you anymore. You've got your life, your career, everything."

Laura thought of her father's latest offer, to use *Montana Men* as a premium for his customers. The hell of it was, she was tempted to go along with the idea. "They still try, Laura," she said. "Believe me, they still try."

WHEN SHE RETURNED to the ranch, Cleo called Bozeman and arranged for a rental convertible to be delivered. She should have reserved a car in the first place, she thought. Bernie had thought she'd get lost out here in the wilds, but she'd begun using the mountains to guide her in the same way she used the Chrysler Building and the Empire State Building in New York.

Of course, if she'd driven herself from Bozeman to the Whispering Winds, she would have missed seeing the pair of bald eagles. But she also would have missed that first intoxicating dose of Tom, and maybe she wouldn't have become so enamored of him so quickly.

She threw herself into her work, photographing Jose shirtless, his arm looped over the neck of a dark bay gelding. It was obvious from the expression she saw through her camera lens that Jose was no gelding, however. He was currently unattached, so Cleo put a star next to the interview notes, indicating Jose was a potential husband candidate.

Except for Tom, there was no one else on the Whispering Winds she wanted to photograph, so for the next several days she toured the neighboring ranches. She soon became known as the "camera lady," and cowboys began to seek her out and offer themselves as candidates. She had to gently reject a few, but she ended up with a good list of prospects, both for the calendar and for her matrimonial scheme. Stu, a red-haired wrangler with great buns, got a star, as did Bo, who was part Native American and had a mysterious sexuality that Cleo knew would drive women crazy. He could probably drive her crazy, too, she thought, if she could get Tom off her mind.

In trying to accomplish that, she stayed away from the Whispering Winds as much as possible. Several evenings she stopped for dinner at a steak house a few miles south of the ranch and didn't park her convertible beside her little cabin until bedtime. On one such occasion, when she'd put in a particularly long day and only wanted to get home and relax, she returned to her car after dinner and discovered it wouldn't start.

"Hey, camera lady!"

She glanced up to see Robert Henderson coming out of the restaurant. He was one of the cowboys she'd had to reject for the calendar because his round baby face wouldn't have photographed well.

"Looks like you got car problems," Robert said.

She smiled at him. "I'm afraid so."

"It's a rental, isn't it?"

"Yep."

"I could try to fix it, but you might get in trouble with the rental agency. Why don't I give you a lift to the Whispering Winds, and you can call the company from there? Let them deal with it."

"Great idea. And thanks."

Robert questioned her endlessly about life in New York for the entire drive home. By the time he finally dropped her off, and she'd thanked him profusely, she was completely drained. Nothing sounded better than a good night's sleep, unless...she glimpsed the row of decorative path lights that led behind her cottage to the area that contained a hot tub she had yet to use.

Moments later she slipped off her bathrobe in the privacy of the darkened forest, took her candy bar out of the robe pocket and mounted the steps to the steaming hot tub. She deserved this, she thought, climbing into the bubbling water with a sigh of contentment. She'd been working damn hard, and as always when she was in the midst of a project, the sexual frustration was building with each photo shoot.

As she settled onto a smooth bench and water swirled over her breasts, she sighed again. Somewhere in the darkness an owl hooted and a small creature scrabbled through the underbrush. Cleo leaned back and rested her head against the wood as she munched her chocolate. She was too tired to care what lurked in the forest. Unless Trixie started going crazy, she refused to worry about bears or cougars.

She just wanted the warm, bubbling water to ease her fatigue and mellow out the sharp edge of her desire. Damn that Tom McBride, anyway. Always before, her sexual hunger had been unfocused, but now, instead of longing for some anonymous lover, she wanted Tom.

She compared every cowboy she photographed to him, and she found every one wanting.

Sliding in deeper, she murmured with delight. She'd been in Jacuzzis before, but never in natural hot springs. The soothing mineral water and the dim glow from the path lights coaxed her gently into an almost hypnotic state. "Don't fall asleep and drown, Griffin," she muttered to herself as her eyes threatened to close.

Yet there was an erotic nature to the experience that kept her on the edge of awareness. Maybe it was being outside, with the scent of pines and the soft whisper of the wind that made her feel a primitive oneness with nature. Finally she gave in to the mood, closed her eyes and allowed herself to drift closer and closer to sleep.

On the outer edge of consciousness, she sensed the presence of another, but felt no alarm, no thrill of danger. Floating in a fantasy world, she imagined that a warm breeze touched her eyelids, then her cheeks, and finally her mouth. The breeze became a brush of lips, and she didn't question, didn't open her eyes. For she knew. He was here.

9

TOM HAD SPENT the last few days stringing fence with Stan. He'd given himself the relentless task to keep thoughts of Cleo at bay, and his muscles were complaining. He'd noticed that Cleo didn't hang around the ranch much, either, and he figured she was trying to avoid him as much as he was trying to avoid her.

When he didn't see her convertible parked beside her cabin that evening, he assumed she was out again, as usual.

He didn't like thinking about that, but he couldn't exactly stop her activities, whatever they might be. The night had turned out to be fairly warm for Montana, so at least he could pamper his aching muscles by taking a nice long soak in the hot tub going to waste behind her cabin. He'd walked down the path from the ranch house wearing only his jeans and boots, with a towel slung over his bare shoulder.

When he reached the clearing, he'd stopped in amazement, wondering if he'd started seeing visions in his desperation for a woman he couldn't have. But no, she was real enough. Maybe something had happened to her convertible and she'd gotten a lift back to the ranch.

He could tell she had no idea he was standing there. Her eyes were closed, and the sound of bubbling water had muffled his footsteps on the path. If he could have conjured up the most tempting image of Cleo he could imagine, this would be it. He'd always been intrigued with the way a woman piled her hair haphazardly on top of her head when she planned to soak in a tub. He found it endearing the way little tendrils fell out of that sort of arrangement, and how kissable a woman's neck seemed, when all her hair was pulled away to expose her soft skin.

Her shoulders were bare, and he suspected the rest of her was, too. After all, she'd announced that was the way she liked hot tubbing, and so did he, for that matter. He should turn around and walk back up that path and leave her to her solitary soak. He should...but even before he started across the little clearing, he knew he'd lost the willpower.

She didn't stir as he undressed and climbed slowly into the swirling water. He remembered how she'd seemed to play possum when he thought she was asleep that morning a few days ago at the campsite. She could be doing that now. A woman as headstrong as Cleo might have to pretend she was in a helpless trance before she could drop her defenses. Yet on some level, she knew what was happening, and she trusted him. He wouldn't betray that.

The steam surrounding them carried the citrus scent of her cologne, and he breathed deep as he eased down beside her on the wooden bench. Her face was flushed from the warmth of the water and her mouth curved slightly, on the brink of a smile. He leaned over and allowed his breath to caress her face. The barest of sighs parted her lips.

His heartbeat thundering in his ears, he touched his mouth to hers with the lightness of snow falling. Her lips were pliant and warm...receptive. Her mouth tasted of chocolate, and he smiled. She'd been snacking again. He sought firmer contact, and she responded, opening to him, inviting him deeper. He followed where she led, desire throbbing within him at the blatant suggestion of her kiss.

Yet his feathery touch betrayed no urgency as he trailed a finger down her throat and felt her pulse hammering in concert with his. For many long moments he stroked her throat, her shoulders, the nape of her neck, as if he were gentling a skittish filly. At last, when he felt she was ready for it, he slipped his hand beneath the water and cradled her breast. He captured her soft moan against his mouth as he continued his slow assault.

Ah, but the weight of her breast felt good in his palm. Her nipple was already taut with passion, as he'd thought it might be. As he stroked his thumb back and forth across the pebbled tip, he loved hearing the subtle hitch in her breathing.

Drawing out the newest stage of his seduction, he fondled her breasts, kneading and stroking as he lazily explored the moist recesses of her mouth with his tongue. Laying his hand over her heart, he could read the tumult he'd created as her chest pounded against his palm. Slowly, so as not to break the connection, he slid his lips away from hers. Her eyes remained closed, but her lashes fluttered. Her lips were parted, swollen from his kisses, and her breath came in agitated little puffs. Ah, Cleo.

Resisting the urge to return to the wonders of her mouth, he followed a path along her jaw and down her throat. He reached the surface of the water and lifted her breast until the water foamed just over the surface of her skin. With flicks of his tongue, he teased her nipple in tandem with the bubbling water, gratified with the way she trembled in his steady grip. At last he drew her, moist and quivering, into his mouth.

She gasped and arched upward, bringing both breasts out of the water. He needed no more invitation than that. Cupping her with both hands, he tasted and savored, raking her gently with his teeth, laving her with his tongue. Touching him for the first time, she combed her damp fingers through his hair and held his head, silently urging him on.

When she began to whimper, he returned to kiss her whimpers away. Then he slid his hand slowly downward, parting her thighs. He marveled that she gave him no resistance. Taking her would be so easy. And such a mistake. She was swollen and ready as he slipped his fingers deep inside. He shook with the need to bury himself there, protection or no protection. But the consequences could bring him to his knees.

So he would settle for this—stroking her until she quivered and arched, touching her until she cried out and exploded in his arms. Perhaps this was all they'd ever share. He wouldn't think beyond this moment, which had appeared like a precious gift.

He lifted his head and spoke for the first time. "Open your eyes, Cleo."

She shook her head. Her breath came fast and shallow.

He pushed in deep and stilled the movement of his hand. "Feel how close I am, Cleo?"

She nodded.

"You let me touch the fire deep inside you," he murmured, kissing her jaw, her cheeks. "Let me see the fire in your eyes when I take you over the edge."

Slowly her eyes opened, pale yet glowing in the dim light of the clearing.

His breath caught in his throat. He'd maintained control of his grinding need to take her fully...until now.

Now he wanted it all—the joining, the pleasure, the sweet release, the mating. From a nearby ridge a wolf howled, and the primitive cry echoed in his heart.

But he was a man, not a wolf. He would finish this and leave without taking what his body screamed to have. He increased the pressure, quickened the rhythm and watched with a fierce sense of possession as the flame leaped in her eyes.

"Yes," he whispered as he felt the contractions begin. Whether she knew it or not, he was staking a claim tonight.

Her eyes darkened. With a soft cry of surrender she lifted her hips, allowing him even deeper penetration as she shook with the force of her climax. He kissed her, plunging his tongue into her mouth as he absorbed her convulsions.

Gradually, she relaxed in his arms. He could bring her to the brink again, he knew. She was ready for more, and the slightest movement of his fingers would be enough to start all over again. She might be able to take it, but he couldn't.

He withdrew his hand, gave her one last lingering kiss and climbed out of the hot tub.

"Tom?" Her voice was dusky with spent passion.

Between being wet and aroused, he had a hell of a time getting his pants on, but he managed that and his boots, too. If he didn't get dressed, he wouldn't be able to look at her without wanting to jump back in and finish the job good and proper, the way it was meant to be done.

"You're...leaving?" she murmured. "But..."

He slung his towel over his shoulder and glanced at her. For a brief second he considered pulling her out of that tub and sitting her on the edge while he unfastened his jeans and...no. He wasn't taking those kinds of chances.

"I'm leaving," he said.

"But you didn't..."

He gazed at her. "A smart cowboy lets a filly get used to him before he tries to ride her for the first time." Then he turned and walked as best he could up the path. As an exit line, it was one of his more clever ones, he thought. Apparently, Cleo didn't appreciate it, though. A heaved stone landed somewhere behind him on the path. Maybe she wasn't as grateful as he thought she'd be.

CLEO HAD NO IDEA how she'd face Tom again. She slept like a zombie that night, though, and she'd always been an insomniac. She overslept, in fact, and as birds twittered outside and sun streamed through the window, she lay in bed and considered the ramifications of what she'd allowed to happen.

It was a murky ethical question. She'd hadn't actually *slept* with Tom, so technically she should be able to continue her husband hunt without feeling guilty. Oh, sure. What kind of woman would allow one man to caress her so intimately that she'd probably never forget the experience, and then within days ask another man if he'd be interested in marriage?

Maybe on this trip she could narrow down the prospects. Then in a few weeks she'd come back to Montana, staying somewhere else, of course, and look up the cowboy she'd set her sights on. In order to approach him with a clear conscience, she needed to put some distance between herself and the hot-tub incident.

As for photographing Tom for the calendar, she hadn't quite broken her rule there, either, but she couldn't imagine being able to maintain her professional demeanor after what they'd shared. Maybe *shared* was the wrong word. He'd played her like a concert pianist seated at a grand piano. It had been... awesome.

She threw back the covers and leaped out of bed. If she stayed there thinking about Tom's hands on her, she'd be in the same state in no time, and that would never do. Then she stood in the middle of the floor, astounded at her behavior. She never leaped out of bed. Crawling out, complaining every inch of the way, was more her style.

She stretched her arms over her head and smiled.

What she'd let happen in the hot tub was ill-advised, but she'd never felt better in her whole life. And she'd never felt less like shooting sexy cowboys. Maybe today would be the best time to take a roll of Juanita's kids, while the rental-car company sorted out what they wanted to do about her disabled convertible.

Dressing quickly, she kept an eye out for Tom as she went up to the back door of the ranch's kitchen and rapped gently. "Juanita?"

Juanita came to the screen door and opened it immediately. "Where have you been keeping yourself? You haven't been sneaking food from the kitchen in days!"

"I'd like to sneak some now," Cleo said. "I'm starving."

"Coming right up." Juanita motioned her inside and went over to open the pantry. "You look good." Her back to Cleo, she pulled out the makings for French toast. "Did you get some good news or something?"

Cleo made a mental note to tone down her pleased expression. She especially didn't want that look on her face if Tom showed up. "Oh, I guess I'm just enjoying the morning. Do you know if—uh—Tom or anybody is around?"

"Tom rode out of here before breakfast." Juanita whipped eggs and milk together. "Did you need him for anything?"

"No! I mean, no. My car broke down last night at the Diamond Bar Steak House, and I —"

"He'd be glad to help you with that, I'm sure, but he didn't say when he'd be back."

"That's okay. I can handle it." She was afraid she sounded as distracted as she felt. "In fact, why don't I go call the rental company while the French toast is cooking?"

"Sure." Juanita gave her a strange look. "How'd you get home last night, then?"

"A cowboy gave me a lift. It worked out fine." Although Cleo knew that Juanita couldn't possibly figure out what happened after that, she still wanted to change the subject. "Listen, after breakfast, I thought I might try a few shots of the kids."

"Oh." Juanita looked bereft. "They're with their father. He took them down to the Gallatin River to fish today. If I'd known that you—"

"Never mind," Cleo said quickly. "I'll catch them another time."

"But you're so busy. And now that you haven't needed snacks during the day because you've been gone so much, I was afraid that you'd decide not to do it."

"I absolutely am going to do it." Cleo had been lukewarm about the idea before, but now that she understood how significant it was to Juanita, she'd make certain the job was accomplished. "Don't worry. I'll be around for a few more days. We'll find time."

Juanita kept pummeling the eggs and milk with the wire whisk, even though the mixture was frothy already. "Jeeter told me how much you paid him to take his picture. I...might have asked too big a favor, just in trade for a few meals. I'll bet you charge a lot for portraits, don't you?"

Cleo walked over and put her hands on Juanita's plump shoulders. "You let me into your kitchen," she said with a smile. "I figure that's beyond price."

Juanita stared at her for a minute, and finally her expression cleared and she grinned. "That's true. Go make your phone call while I fix you the best French toast west of the Mississippi."

Fifteen minutes later, her mouth full of the lightest, sweetest French toast she'd ever eaten, Cleo had to agree with her. She sat where Juanita had set her a place, on a stool drawn up to the butcher-block island in the center of the large kitchen. Juanita poured herself a cup of coffee and pulled up a stool to join her.

Cleo savored the bite a moment longer before swallowing it. "Tom is a lucky man," she said.

"Oh, I wouldn't say that."

"Why not? He's got this beautiful ranch, a fantastic cook and loyal hands to help him run the place."

"Assuming he can hang on."

Cleo took a sip of coffee so wonderful that it would set the standard for her from now on. "Are things really that bad? He mentioned something during the cattle drive about finances, but then he shrugged it off."

"He'd hate for me to talk to you about it."

"But you're dying to talk to somebody," Cleo guessed.

"I'm worried sick, to tell you the truth." Juanita waved at Cleo's plate. "Keep eating. I'll talk. You eat."

"You don't have to coax me. This is outstanding." Cleo pushed the edge of her fork through a golden slice of French toast dripping with maple syrup. "And I promise that whatever you say goes no further."

"I know that." Juanita cradled her mug of coffee. "I have good instincts. Take that Deidre. I knew from the minute he brought her here she would be bad news."

"I heard what she did to Tom."

Juanita's brown eyes turned almost black with anger. "It was bad enough that she did it, but not even to tell him beforehand, to give him a chance to stop her...that was evil. Especially after all the money he wasted flying to New York once a month because he figured it was only fair that he do part of the traveling. Then when they split up, he had to pay her a cash settlement because he's the one who asked for the divorce, and Tom's not the type to sign a prenuptial agreement. He was already stretched pretty thin after buying his sister out, and then his dad's doctor bills started coming in."

"Wow. That does sound bad."

"I've pieced all this together on my own, but I see him in his office, hunched over the books. Unless he's got some gold buried somewhere on the ranch, he's in big trouble."

"You mean, he might lose the ranch?"

Juanita gazed at her. "It happens all the time around here. Ranching's tough, and taking in guests helps keep you even. But let an ex-wife take you to the cleaners, or let medical bills cut into your profits, and it's *adiós, muchachos*."

"But this has been McBride land for five generations!"

Juanita nodded. "Can you imagine how that weighs on him? And he worries about all of us. I could get another job, but I don't want another one. I love this place as much as if it was my family that had been here for five generations. The first time I laid eyes on it, I recognized it as a real place, one that gets in your blood."

Cleo finished her meal and picked up her coffee mug. She knew what Juanita meant. She also knew that it didn't apply to any apartment she'd ever lived in in Manhattan. She felt a connection with the city in general, but it was far less personal than the one Tom had with the Whispering Winds.

She sent Juanita a rueful glance. "I thought if he'd just agree to pose for me, I could help him out. Sounds like that would be a drop in the bucket."

"Yes." Juanita smiled. "Although I'd give anything to see what you could do with him in a calendar pose. He has no idea what a sexy guy he is."

Cleo felt the heat rise to her cheeks.

"Aha!" Juanita set down her mug with a bang. "So I was right!"

Cleo stood and picked up her plate. "I really have to get going. I'm sure you have plenty to do before lunch. I—"

"I see you two ending up together, you know."

Cleo dumped her plate in the sink and ran water over it. She kept her back to Juanita. "That's ridiculous, and you know it. My life is in New York, just like Deidre's was. Even if Tom and I are somewhat attracted to each other, which you've obviously noticed, we'd both be crazy to act on it."

"You're no more like Deidre than I'm like Cruella De Ville."

"Tom thinks I'm like Deidre," Cleo said softly.

"Then Tom needs to look a little closer."

Cleo turned, bracing both hands behind her on the counter. "I am like her. I put my career ahead of everything else. Marriage, kids, a home—they're all secondary, just like with Deidre. I've worked hard to get where I am, and I don't intend to give it up."

Juanita gazed at her, her expression serene. "If you say so."

"I do. In fact, I need to use the telephone again, so I can call my assistant. Business is on my mind all the time."

"Uh-huh."

"It is, Juanita." She started out of the kitchen. "Thanks for a wonderful breakfast."

"Anytime."

Cleo had nothing specific to discuss with Bernie, but she needed to connect with that part of her life. She felt her grip on it slipping.

"How's the manhunt going?" Bernie asked cheerfully.

"I, uh, may have to make two trips to get the job accomplished," Cleo admitted. "It *is* pretty tough to get something like that settled in two weeks."

"Can't you find anybody who dreams of connubial bliss in a hotel room?"

"Stop it, Bernie. Honestly, you're sounding so old-fashioned. Did you get the rolls of film I shipped?"

"Of course. The contact sheets are on their way. You've got some cuties there. If I didn't have George, I might consider a guest-ranch vacation, myself."

"Yeah, there's something about cowboys." Especially one in particular, she thought.

"I have to ask. Are any of the ones on the rolls I saw husband candidates?"

"No." The answer came out too quickly, and there was no logic behind it, only emotion generated by a passionate man in a hot tub. She just couldn't think about marriage so soon after that. "I mean, probably not."

"I counted eight guys. If you've eliminated eight of your thirteen, you're not giving yourself much leeway."

"That's why I need another trip out here."

"That reservation wasn't easy to get," Bernie said. "You have some free time in September, so why don't I just schedule you at the same—"

"No!"

"What's the problem? You seemed to like it well enough in the beginning."

"It's okay. I just want to...branch out. Listen, don't schedule anything until I get back."

"All right. You sound funny. Is something wrong?"

Cleo cleared her throat. "Not a thing."

"You father called again. He wants an answer on whether he can count on the calendar as a premium."

"Tell him he can."

"Cleo, are you sure? You sound a little stressed, and bringing your father in on the project probably isn't—"

"I can handle it. In fact, I want to handle it. I've waited a long time for him to take me seriously. Now that he has, it would be childish to refuse."

Bernie sighed. "Okay. See you soon."

"Right. We'll take an afternoon off and go shopping on Fifth Avenue."

"We'll do *what?*"

"Go shopping," Cleo said. "Do lunch at the Four Seasons."

"You've never suggested a shopping trip in all the years we've known each other. What's up?"

"I just realized I'm not as appreciative of New York as I should be. Just because we don't have high mountains and moose and eagles and stuff doesn't mean we don't have lots of cool things in New York."

"Uh, okay, Cleo. Whatever you say. Shopping. Right. I gotta go now, toots. The other line's ringing. And the next time one of those cowboys rolls you a cigarette, ask what's in it. Sounds to me the mountains aren't the only thing that's high in Montana."

10

CLEO DID FEEL a little high after last night's episode. Compounding her sense of disorientation was having nothing to do. She'd always been in a rush, always on a schedule, but the rental-car situation wouldn't be straightened out for at least a couple of hours, so she had no wheels. She couldn't photograph Juanita's kids, and the phone call to Bernie had only used up a few minutes.

After a quick trip back to the kitchen for carrot chunks, she wandered down to the corral. Dynamite stood in the same sleepy-eyed position she'd been in when Cleo first saw her the morning of the cattle drive.

"Sandbagger," Cleo said. She clucked to the horse and reached in her pocket for a piece of carrot. "You just want everybody to think you're old and tired so they won't make you work too hard."

Dynamite walked over, and Cleo slipped her the carrot. She tried not to make a big deal about it and attract the attention of the other horses in the corral, although there weren't many. Jeeter had taken a big group out on a trail ride this morning, along with Trixie. She'd seen them head out as she walked up to the house for breakfast.

"Want to take her out for a spin?" Jose asked, ambling up to her with a posthole digger over his shoulder.

"Are you offering to go along?"

"Wish I could, but the boss needs some posts set this morning. That doesn't mean you can't take a ride by yourself. It's a great day for it."

The idea appealed to her. "Aren't you afraid I'll get lost?"

"Find a fence and follow along. It'll lead you back home. Go out for about an hour, turn around and come back. I've seen you ride. You'll be fine."

"Okay, I'll go. Let me get my camera."

"I'll saddle Dynamite for you."

"I'll do that, too," Cleo said. "If I'm going out by myself, the least I can do is saddle my own horse."

Jose smiled at her. "Good for you."

She studied him and wondered if maybe he could be the one, after all. He was very handsome, and a nice guy. "Do you plan on having kids some day?" she asked. She hadn't figured out how to work that into the photo-shoot interview.

He blinked. "Excuse me?"

"Kids." Cleo managed a laugh. "Don't ask me why I thought of that, but I did."

Jose cleared his throat. "First I reckon I'd better find the right lady. Some of that decision would be up to her."

"What if she didn't want any?"

"Look, if you're trying to set me up with somebody in particular, then tell me who it is, and we can—"

"Nope. Just idle curiosity."

He swung the posthole digger from his shoulder and leaned on it, gazing at her in speculation. "Well, I've never considered that question, but it would depend on why she didn't want them, I guess. I'd understand a medical problem, or maybe she's worried about over-population, or the cost of college, things like that. But I always figured on being a father some day. Giving that up would be a sacrifice, and I wouldn't make it without a powerful reason."

"I see." That took care of Jose as a candidate.

He grinned. "And I still say you have somebody in mind you want to marry me off to. Send her on out. I'll change her mind about the kid thing."

Cleo waved her hands in front of her. "Nobody, really. I'll be right back with my camera."

"Don't forget your hat," he called out after her.

SOMETIME LATER, her hat firmly in place, Cleo guided Dynamite along a barbed-wire fence as it angled away from the ranch. She took a deep breath and smelled freedom, just as she had on the morning of the cattle drive. Out here there was no phone, no fax, no expectations.

She wondered where Tom was right now. Not that she'd ridden out here hoping to find him. In fact, he was the last person on earth she wanted to run into. But after last night, she'd rather their next encounter be in private, instead of when other people were around. Now that she knew Juanita had picked up on the attraction between the two of them, she was afraid others might do the same.

The longer she rode, the less any of that seemed to matter. She glanced at her watch and knew she'd better turn back, but she hated to do it just yet. Dynamite would accelerate on the way home, anyway, and the ride was so therapeutic. The majesty of her surroundings dwarfed human concerns. She remembered what

Tom had called it—*the most beautiful office in the world.*
Yet he might lose it. She didn't want to think about that.
Tom belonged here, and the idea that he might lose the
right to ride through this country really bothered her.

She leaned forward to pat Dynamite's soft neck. "It
won't happen, will it, Dynamite? The Whispering
Winds will be McBride land for a long time yet, right?"

The mare's ears twitched back in acknowledgment of
the conversation.

"You're a good pony, Dynamite. I'm going to miss
you. In fact, I'm going to take your picture so I'll have
something to remember you by." Pulling the mare to a
halt beside the fence, she dismounted and dropped the
reins to the ground, as Tom had instructed everyone to
do during the cattle drive.

She walked a slight distance away, trying different
camera angles. The horse stood in her typical half-
asleep pose, looking like one disreputable nag. Cleo
tried snapping her fingers, but nothing happened.
"Open your eyes, Dynamite," she ordered. Then she remembered those had been Tom's exact words to her last
night. She'd wanted to stay one step removed from
what was happening in that hot tub. If she didn't open
her eyes, she wasn't truly acknowledging that it was
Tom there with her, touching her in all those forbidden
ways. But he'd appealed to her sense of justice, and
she'd opened her eyes, only to find herself drowning in
the experience he was giving her.

Gazing into his eyes during those final moments of
pleasure, she'd had the unmistakable feeling that he
was binding her to him. That was ridiculous, of course.
She wasn't bound to anyone. She was going back home
soon, and putting together a calendar that would be her

biggest hit yet. Sphinx Cosmetics would help make it so.

She crouched in the grass. "Okay, you sorry piece of horseflesh. If you don't perk up, all of New York will see what a lazy bag of bones you are, and they'll never believe you're the queen of the cow ponies. Is this the image you want carried to the Big Apple?"

Amazingly, Dynamite's ears flicked forward and she looked suddenly alert.

"Hey, that's more like it!" Cleo clicked the shutter.

Dynamite tossed her head and rolled her eyes.

"Go, baby! They're gonna love you on Broadway, sweetheart!"

Cleo kept shooting as Dynamite grew increasingly more animated, snorting and shaking her head. But when the mare let out a piercing scream and reared, Cleo decided something was wrong.

"Hey, leave that stuff to Trigger, okay, girl?" Taking the camera from around her neck and laying it on the ground, Cleo edged toward Dynamite, who reared again, coming down stiff-legged. The mare's eyes rolled as she reared once more, and Cleo's throat tightened with fear. She wondered if the camera had spooked Dynamite. Yet that didn't make much sense. Whatever had happened, Cleo had to get the horse calmed down.

She spoke in a low, soothing voice. "Look, if that little black box upsets you, we don't have to take any more pictures. I didn't mean to get you so worked up. Talk about camera-shy. You and your owner are two of a kind."

Dynamite seemed to pay no attention as she continued to rear, trampling the grass in front of her.

"Easy, girl." Cleo decided if she could get close enough to grab the reins, she could keep the horse from rearing, at least, and maybe work her out of the fit she'd thrown herself into. She reached cautiously toward the dangling reins.

And saw the snake.

Or what was left of it. The mangled carcass had once been a snake, but the torn-up mess that Dynamite had made of it caused Cleo to turn away and clutch her stomach.

Finally she took a deep breath and gathered the courage to survey the situation. Dynamite had stopped pounding the earth and backed up several steps. She stood quivering, her flanks heaving from the effort. Cleo made herself look closer at the carnage on the ground. She'd never seen a rattler before, but the tail of this snake was still intact, and it resembled the pictures she'd seen on television and in books.

Cleo began to shiver as she gazed at Dynamite. "I think you might have just saved my life, sweetheart. I probably walked right past that thing, greenhorn that I am." She glanced back to where she'd left her camera. "I hope they don't travel in pairs. Maybe we'll just ride over and get my camera. You've got a lot more sense about what's around here than I do."

Skirting the mangled snake, she gathered the reins and started to mount. That's when she noticed the barbed wire tangled around Dynamite's left hind leg. A strand had worked loose from the fence. In her frenzy to kill the snake, Dynamite had put her foot right through a loop that had been lying on the ground. Backing up to get away from the snake carcass had only made things worse.

Cleo felt horrible as she crouched to view the damage. Dynamite's leg was bleeding from several places where the barbs had been driven into the skin.

"I didn't see this loose wire, either, girl," she murmured. "I should have been watching the ground, but all I could do was stare at the mountains. You'll probably never want to ride out here with me again, and I wouldn't blame you." She sighed and laid her hat on the ground. "Guess we'd better see about getting you untangled. Let's hope to hell another snake doesn't show up while we're doing that."

With gloves, it would have been a tricky job, she thought. Without gloves, it would take a small miracle to accomplish, but she was out here by herself, with no one else to get her out of this fix. She'd just have to manage.

She got to her knees behind the horse. "Now don't kick me, sweetie," she cautioned, as she checked Dynamite to see if the horse had been bitten. "Ouch!" She pulled her bleeding finger back and stuck it in her mouth. "Damn, but that stuff hurts. I can just imagine what it feels like to have it wrapped around your leg. Easy, baby." Cleo was relieved to find no evidence of snakebite on Dynamite's leg. Now all she had to do was untangle the wire.

Gritting her teeth against the pain as the barbed wire continued to bite her, trying to pretend there were no more snakes within miles and hoping that Dynamite didn't kick her clear into next week, Cleo worked with the tangle. Sweat ran into her eyes and she wiped it away, belatedly realizing that she'd smeared blood from her cut fingers over her face.

She talked to Dynamite the whole time she worked

with the wire to let the horse know exactly where she was, what she was doing and why she'd appreciate it if the mare would stand perfectly still. Once she felt a pair of eyes on her and glanced sideways to find a cottontail sitting beside the fence post staring at her.

"What'dya say, Thumper?"

The little rabbit twitched its nose and hopped away.

"Guess where there are bunnies, there aren't any snakes," she said to Dynamite. "Or at least we can hope, huh? Damn, but this wire hurts. We're getting somewhere, but it's slow going, girl," she said. "I think we're liable to be really late getting home."

ON HIS WAY BACK to the ranch for lunch, Tom stopped by to check Jose's progress with the postholes. "Looks good, Jose," he said, leaning on his saddle horn. "It's about time to knock off for lunch."

Jose took off his hat and wiped his forehead with a bandanna. "Yeah, I know. I thought I'd work until Cleo gets back and see if she wants any help putting away the tack."

The mention of Cleo's name started Tom's heart racing. He was in worse shape than he thought. "Where'd she go?" he asked, trying to sound casual. He wondered if he'd ridden near her this morning and not even known it. Except that he thought he would have known it, somehow. There was an electricity between them that would have alerted him to her presence.

"She took Dynamite out. Headed up along the northwest fence line," Jose said. "After the way she proved herself on the cattle drive, and knowing what a good horse Dynamite is, I figured it would be okay. I told her to follow the fence so she wouldn't get lost."

Tom nodded. "Sounds fine to me. When's she due in?"

Jose tilted his hat back and gazed up at the sun. "I'm expecting her any minute. She probably started taking pictures and forgot the time. She'll be along."

"So she's later than you thought she'd be?" He tried not to think in terms of disaster but couldn't seem to help himself. She was a greenhorn. *His* greenhorn.

"I guess she's a little late," Jose admitted. "Not enough to be worried about, though." He glanced at Tom. "We had a real strange conversation before she left. She asked if I wanted kids, and what I'd do if the woman I planned to marry didn't want any."

"Did she?"

"Yeah. I think she wants to fix me up with somebody."

"Could be." *And her name better not be Cleo*, he thought grimly. He'd be damned if another man would end up with her. "I think I'll ride up that way and see her home," he said, acting as if he'd just thought of it. He'd known from the minute Jose said where she'd gone that he'd go up and meet her. He'd done a lot of thinking this morning, and he and Cleo needed to talk.

"Okay," Jose said. "But I'm sure she's fine. She's a smart lady."

"That's for sure. Tell Juanita not to expect me for lunch." He wheeled Red and started off toward the fence line. Once he was out of Jose's sight, he kicked the horse into a gallop.

"THAT DOES IT, sweetheart." Cleo eased the last curl of wire from around the horse's leg and tossed the strand back toward the fence post. Her fingers ached and were covered with blood, both hers and Dynamite's. Her shoulders and legs were cramped from hunching in one position for so long. When she tried to stand, the blood roared in her ears and she was afraid she might pass out.

"Just give me a minute, Dynamite," she said, flopping back onto the grass and closing her eyes as the adrenaline surge that had carried her through the ordeal subsided. "Snakes, stay the hell away. I need a few seconds to rest here."

"Dear God."

At the soft, anguished cry, she opened her eyes and looked up to find Tom leaning over her, his face blanched white.

She'd expected to be embarrassed the first time she saw him again after the hot-tub encounter, but she was too grateful for his presence to waste time on embarrassment. "Hi, Tom," she said. "How's tricks?"

He dropped to his knees beside her, his expression grim. "Don't try to talk. Don't move. Something could be wrong with your back."

She sat up.

"I said don't move, woman!" he bellowed, grabbing her by the shoulders.

"Would you pipe down? You're scaring the horses, and Dynamite's been through enough for one day."

"To hell with Dynamite! She kicked you in the head!"

"No, she didn't. I—"

"Then why are you lying here covered with blood? Or at least, you were lying here." He gripped her more firmly. "Lie down, Cleo."

"Why?" She loved the way he'd ridden to her rescue,

and having him hold her made all the trauma worthwhile. "So you can have your way with me?"

"Dammit, how can you think about sex at a time like this?"

"Because I'm fine."

"You look like the devil."

She supposed so. "I cut my fingers on the barbed wire when I was untangling it from Dynamite's leg. Then I wiped the sweat off my face and got blood on it."

He released her shoulders and picked up both her hands to examine them. "Aw, hell, Cleo. You're all torn up."

"I had to get the barbed wire off. Take a look at her leg, will you, Tom? I think it's mostly surface wounds, but I'm not an expert on these things."

"Don't move." He released her wrists and went to check on Dynamite. Then he came back and crouched in front of Cleo again. He looked into her eyes, his own dark with guilt. "She's not hurt too bad, but we'll ride double on Red, so we don't put any extra strain on her. I should have checked this section of fence today instead of riding off like some idiot this morning."

"Tom, this is not your fault." She suspected his solitary ride this morning had a lot to do with her. "Besides, I'm fine, and Dynamite will heal. The rattlesnake, now, that's a different story."

"The rattlesnake?" His gaze sharpened. "Are you bit?"

"No, thanks to Dynamite. She trampled it while I was engrossed in taking her picture. Big old snake, too. I wondered why she became so alert. Then when she reared—"

"You're sure it's dead?"

"Go look. About a yard in front of Dynamite you'll find what's left of it."

"Stay right there and don't move while I check it out."

"Okay." She was through trying to convince him she wasn't hurt. As soon as he stood up and walked away, she got to her feet and dusted herself off. After picking up her hat and tapping it against her thigh, she put it on and moved around to Dynamite's head. Wrapping an arm around the mare's neck, she scratched between the animal's ears. "You did great, sweetheart. Thanks for killing the snake, and not kicking me, and being the best horse on the planet." She gave the mare a kiss on the nose.

"Is that your idea of staying put?"

She turned and saw him standing with her camera in his hand.

"I found this lying in the grass," he said. "Knowing how much it means to you, I'm impressed that you left it to take care of your horse."

Cleo stroked the mare's neck. "The truth is, I love this little mare. I know she's technically yours, but we bonded today, so I feel as if she's a little bit my horse now."

"I understand." A faint smile touched his mouth and he shook his head. "But damned if you don't look like a massacre victim, Cleo." He handed her the camera and took her by the arm. "Come on, let me clean up your hands and face a little before we ride back, or you'll give everybody a heart attack."

"Was it a rattlesnake?"

He led her over to his horse. "It was. Timber rattler. Good-sized. Most of the time they go about their business and don't bother anyone. You had the bad luck to stop in the wrong place."

"And I didn't look around, Tom. If I had, I might have seen the snake, and I certainly would have seen the barbed wire. I should have picked a different place to take Dynamite's picture."

"Don't be too hard on yourself." He opened his saddlebag. "I can stow the camera in here if you want."

"Sure. Thanks. I really do feel like an idiot, though, Tom. Jose sent me out with such confidence, and I made a mess of things."

"Hey, you're new to this country." Pulling a red bandanna from his hip pocket, he wet it with water from his canteen. "You're not expected to think of everything the first few times. Now let me see those hands."

She held them out and pressed her lips together against the pain while he washed away the blood.

He shook his head. "You're tough, lady. Most people wouldn't have ripped up their hands like this to get that barbed wire off."

"I didn't see any alternative."

He frowned as he worked carefully on her wounds. "You could have waited until someone came to get you."

"I wasn't sure when that would be."

"I know," he said gently, glancing up at her. "And I admire your take-charge attitude. You reacted like a real cowgirl."

"Why, thank you." She smiled.

"God, but you look gruesome. Hold still, and let me get some of that dried blood off your face."

She lifted her face and closed her eyes.

He nudged her hat back on her head, cradled her chin

in one hand and started wiping the cool cloth over her cheeks. "I'm sorry this had to happen to you. You're probably dying to get back to civilization about now."

"Not...exactly." Getting back to civilization was the last thing on her mind. All she could think of was the tenderness of his hand cupping her chin. And how much she wanted him to kiss her. After the trauma with the snake and the barbed wire, she needed to be held, and this was the man she wanted for the job.

Funny how battling for physical survival had rearranged her priorities in no time. Having Tom on the cover of her calendar didn't hold a candle to having him in her arms. New York seemed a million miles away from this sun-drenched meadow and this intriguing man.

"Speaking of things we shouldn't have done," he said. "That business last night..."

"Mmm." Her heart hammered as she replayed every detail. The memory moved through her body, arousing each portion it touched.

"That probably wasn't too bright of me." He'd stopped wiping her face, but he still cupped her face in his hand.

She opened her eyes and gazed up at him. "I don't think intelligence had much to do with it."

He brought his other hand to her face. "You got that right. And it looks like I'm going to keep on being stupid." His lips captured hers with an urgency that took her breath away.

She wrapped her arms around him and hung on to every taut inch of that glorious body. She'd been denied close contact with him the night before, denied the press of his erection and the rapid beat of his heart as he plunged his tongue into her mouth.

Beside them, Red snorted.

Tom lifted his mouth from hers. "We can't stay here. Jose will be coming along any minute to see what happened to us."

She groaned with frustration. "You're right. And we have to get Dynamite home and doctor her cuts."

He smiled. "You really are starting to think like a cowgirl." He kissed her more gently. "We'll settle this matter after we get back to the ranch."

She rubbed against him. "We're riding double all the way home, huh?"

"If I can survive it, we are. Damn, but you get me hot, woman."

Cleo felt her husband-hunting project slipping away, as well. Spending the next few nights with Tom outweighed every other consideration. "Want to do something about that when we get home, cowboy?"

11

DID HE EVER WANT to do something about it, Tom thought as they rode double on Red, with Cleo in the saddle holding the reins and Tom behind her, one arm wrapped around her rib cage just under her breasts, the other grasping Dynamite's lead rope. Her scent filled his nostrils and riding wasn't easy while a guy was aroused, he discovered. He looked longingly at shady glens they passed on the way to the ranch. Pine needles and a horse blanket would do just fine for what he was considering.

But they had to see to Dynamite. Besides, he wanted to discuss a few things with Cleo before he jumped into her bed. He'd managed to avoid giving her a straight answer to her proposition by kissing her hard and hoisting her up on Red. She probably thought that was a yes, when in fact it was a definite maybe.

He liked the way she'd reacted today, assuming responsibility for the accident with Dynamite and doing her best to rectify things. He winced every time he thought about her tender hands on that barbed wire, but he guessed a greenhorn had to earn her spurs somehow. He wondered if she realized how well she was adapting to this country. Then again, maybe she realized it all too well, which had prompted her questions to Jose. Maybe she was planning on roping herself a cowboy before she returned to New York, just like Deidre had done when she'd come to the ranch as a guest.

"Jose said you asked his opinion on a matrimonial issue this morning," he said. He felt the slight tenseness in her body.

"It's good to know my portrait subjects in depth," she said. "The more I know about them, the better job I'll do in choosing the shot that emphasizes their character."

His grip tightened and he leaned forward to murmur into her ear. "The day I picked you up at the airport, you said you don't take any B.S. from folks. Neither do I, and that last explanation was chock-full of it."

She shivered. "Don't breathe on my ear like that."

He blew softly. "Why not?"

"It gets me...worked up."

He rotated his forearm so he could cup her breast. "We might as well both be in that condition."

"Tom." It was more of a sigh than a command for him to stop.

So he didn't. He just kept his hand there, lazily stroking her breast. "Are you going to tell me why you asked Jose whether he wants to have kids after he gets married?"

She sighed again, deeper this time. "I might as well. The plan is in shambles, anyway, thanks to you."

"Oh?" He kept his tone level, his caress light, but his body went on alert at the word *plan*. "And what was your plan, sweetheart?"

"To find a husband."

He went totally still. "Is that right?"

"Don't worry. I wasn't after you."

He wanted to hit something and curse a blue streak. "You were after Jose," he said, his throat tight. He wondered how far things had gone between the two of them. He'd hate to have to fire the wrangler, but he'd do it.

"Not specifically Jose. And especially not after I found out how much he wants children."

Tom's head began to spin. "I don't get it."

"You're not going to like it, either, but please try to understand. You saw firsthand how shooting a calendar picture affects me. I...need somebody I can depend on, somebody to...work that out of my system so I don't end up seducing one of my subjects someday."

"Seems like you could hire that done," he said with more than a trace of bitterness.

"I was afraid you'd have that reaction. But it's more than sex, really. I need a friend, somebody in my corner, a person to be with during the lonely downtimes of the business. I'm looking for someone who doesn't think in rigid terms about what marriage is, someone who would consider a commuter marriage. We wouldn't even have to live together, just meet every couple of weeks."

"And get it on." Her concept of marriage horrified him, but damned if her idea wasn't also the most provocative one he'd ever come across.

"Well, I hope we'll also enjoy each other's company, but basically, I guess that's the bottom line."

"That isn't marriage. That's sex."

"I disagree. There would be love, and mutual respect, and commitment. I realize it's a little unusual, but that's what I need, and that's what I wanted to work toward on this trip. And then I met you."

"I still don't get it." He was beginning to understand,

though. He just wanted her to lay it out for him so there could be no misunderstandings later.

"You told me right away you weren't interested in marriage," she said. "And even if you were, I can't imagine you agreeing to that arrangement."

"That's for damn sure. A guy would have to be a wimp to go for that deal. Like a puppy on a string."

She pushed his hand away from her breast. "Or a more flexible one than you are."

He snorted. "Like a pretzel, more likely."

"You can make fun of my idea all you want. Your opinion doesn't really matter. In fact, you have nothing to do with my plan, except..."

"Except what?"

"Except that I don't feel right looking for a husband when you and I have shared...certain moments."

"I see." Her standards were offbeat, but at least she had some, he thought. "Maybe I wasn't so dumb to climb in that hot tub, after all, if I've kept you from making a damn parlor pet out of one of our fine Montana boys."

"I don't know why I'm attracted to you, to be honest. You're way too macho for my tastes. If I was smart, I'd stay completely away from you."

"You said intelligence has nothing to do with it."

"I guess not. The minute you touch me, I don't have a brain cell working."

He pulled her close again. "The rest of you sure hums right along, though."

"Yes, it certainly does." She sighed and snuggled back against him.

Oh, God, he was in trouble. He was already imagining himself in her cabin this afternoon, making love in her king-size bed. Yet if he did that, he'd be dancing to her tune, providing a temporary physical release. He was worth more than that, and so was she. He just had to figure out a way to make her see how insulting her plan was to both of them.

She'd never be happy with a lapdog for a husband. She wasn't a halfway kind of person, no matter what she attempted. He'd seen that on the cattle drive and again when she did what she had to do for Dynamite just now. She needed somebody as strong as she was, someone who expected her to give herself completely to the relationship. Someone like...him. Not that he was interested in a career woman from New York who didn't want kids.

The hell he wasn't. She might be from New York, but Montana fit her personality like a glove. He would fit her like a glove. And as for kids, she'd love those, too. She just didn't know it yet.

"So I was wondering," she said, her voice low and sultry, "if you have some free time this afternoon?"

"I might." Even knowing he planned to throw a monkey wrench into her plans, he still felt his blood heat at the temptation she held out. "Don't you have some pictures to take or something?"

"I had an appointment, but my car gave out last night, and I don't know if it's fixed yet."

"What if it is?"

"I could pretend it wasn't."

She'd alter her schedule for him, he realized. That was telling, in itself. "How many more cowboys do you have to round up for this project?"

"I have eight so far."

"Then you need four more." An idea was forming, and he let it simmer for a while.

"I guess that's all I need now. I'd planned to find thirteen, so if one of them worked out as a husband, I could eliminate him from the calendar and still have twelve."

He blew out a breath. She'd apparently thought it would be that simple. She'd spent so much time behind a camera that she had no idea how the world worked. "And you really expected to get away with that?"

"Apparently I won't. Not on this trip, at any rate."

"I think having thirteen possibilities for your calendar is a good idea, anyway, in case somebody doesn't work out."

"Oh, they'll all work out. I screen my subjects pretty carefully, and the contract's binding."

"What if a subject didn't want to sign a contract?" he asked carefully.

"Then we wouldn't have a deal."

"Care to make an exception with me?"

She stiffened in his arms. "Are you saying you'll pose for me, after all?"

"I will, if I don't have to sign a contract until after I've seen the pictures and I can make my decision then."

All snuggling ended as she sat forward. "If there's a chance I can use you as a cover shot, that cancels out...anything between us."

"I guess that's your choice." He had no idea which way she'd go, but either way, he planned to show her that making love wasn't the simple bodily function she imagined. It wasn't a game, and it wasn't a career aid. It was the essence of life itself.

OFFERING TO POSE for the cover was the very last thing Cleo had expected of him. She recovered slowly from the shock as they neared the ranch. The choice was a no-brainer, really. A few times in bed with him, a casual affair that would end once she left Montana, versus a cover photo for her calendar that could guarantee her reputation, an image that would guarantee that the calendar she presented to Sphinx Cosmetics would be the best in her career.

He might deny her the use of the photos, of course, but she doubted it. No subject had ever been unhappy with the way he looked in one of her calendars. She had an eye for the shot that maximized a man's sexual charisma, and they loved seeing that quality reflected back to them. Even Tom, who only used a mirror to shave, would love it.

Looking at the question from Tom's angle, there was no doubt which way to go, either. The calendar could only help his financial situation. He might turn down the modeling contracts and the film deals, but business at the Whispering Winds would increase, especially with Jeeter and Jose in the calendar. Single women would flock to the ranch, and Tom would be able to raise his prices.

The fact that Tom himself would be mobbed with eligible women bothered her a little, but she couldn't allow herself to care about that. She and Tom had no future, and to begrudge him happiness in the arms of another woman was selfish and unfair. Her jaw might clench and plans for murder might run through her mind at the thought of him making love to someone else, but eventually she'd get over it. She'd have to.

She took a deep breath. "Okay, it's a deal. I'll take the

shots and have them developed without a contract. When do you want to schedule a session?"

"Name your time."

"Let me think about it. I have to decide what setting and what kind of light I want to use."

"Just let me know."

She should be jubilant after gaining the prize she'd sought from the moment she'd walked out of the jetway and spied him waiting for her in the terminal. Instead, she wanted to cry. He'd be in front of her camera soon, but she wouldn't be able to feel his warm lips on hers, or his strong arms holding her tight, or his gentle touch ever again. It was more of a sacrifice than she'd counted on.

TIME WAS RUNNING OUT, and Cleo still hadn't figured out where to shoot Tom. Hoping inspiration would strike while she worked, she scheduled sessions with three of the four remaining cowboys. She took Eddie down to the Gallatin River and posed him standing in the water, jeans soaked and molding his lean hips. She got wet herself for that one, and welcomed the cold water on her heated body. Images of making love to Tom kept superimposing themselves over Eddie, but that only seemed to increase the electricity and bring out the best in the dark-haired cowboy, who had no idea she was imagining he was someone else.

She posed Ty in a cowboy bar and had him drink a little of the beer she used for a prop so he'd loosen up. He loosened up beautifully, giving her some great shots and another bad case of sexual frustration. If only Tom hadn't agreed to the cover shot, he could be easing that ache for her, but the cover would make the anguish all worthwhile, she told herself.

With Andy, she insisted he take off his shirt and lie in a field of wildflowers. He'd hated the idea at first, but as usual, Cleo played with his mind until he gazed up at her with exactly the degree of sensuality she wanted from him. When she returned from that shoot, she flung off her clothes and took the coldest shower in history.

That evening she took stock of the eleven poses she'd used so far and realized she still wasn't sure how to pose Tom. When she'd arrived, she'd visualized him leaning against a fence, but that seemed too common now, too much like some of her other portraits for the calendar. The pressure of taking the best photo of her career had cramped her mind, no doubt, but she had to uncramp it, and fast. She had exactly two days left. Two more days of Montana. She tried not to think about that. She could come back to Montana, of course, but not to this ranch. Never again to this ranch.

After a restless night that caused her to oversleep the next morning, she bummed some more carrots from Juanita and headed to the corral to see Dynamite. She'd agreed to shoot Juanita's kids on her last afternoon at the ranch, a relaxing windup to the schedule. She'd have a session with her final cowboy, Jake, in the morning and Juanita's kids in the afternoon. The next morning she'd leave for New York.

That left today and tonight for Tom's cover shot. Leaning against the corral fence, she scratched behind Dynamite's ears and wished for inspiration.

"Seems to me we're running out of time to get that picture taken."

She glanced up as Tom walked toward her. She

hadn't seen him, except from a distance or in her dreams, since the day of the barbed-wire incident. The longing to hold him was so intense that she couldn't speak. Her body hungered for his in a way that made her wonder if she was coming down with something. She felt flushed and dizzy just looking at him.

"I've been waiting for you to let me know," he said softly, leaning an arm against the corral and standing very close to her. "Did you find a better prospect for that cover and decide to pass up my offer?"

"No." She sounded hoarse and nervous. "I just haven't been able to figure out the setting I want to use."

"You should have asked me for suggestions."

She hadn't thought of that. Usually she was reluctant to take ideas from her subjects because they seldom understood the requirements for the shots and then she was in the position of having to reject their suggestion. But she was so totally dry in this case that she decided to risk it with Tom.

"Okay," she said, looking at him from under the brim of her hat—his hat day after tomorrow. "What do you have in mind?"

"My bedroom."

She backed up a step, her pulse racing. "For the photo session, or for...something else?"

"For the photo session. You've made it clear what your rules are. Juanita has quite a collection of your calendars, and I've been studying them. If your aim is the sexual side of the men, why not show one of them in bed?"

"I've always concentrated on the work environment." And in Montana, that meant using the great outdoors, for the most part. "Besides, the light might not be any good in...there." She couldn't bring herself to say *your bedroom*, certain the words would come out sounding the way she felt—jumpy.

"Why not take a look yourself? The windows face south, so the light doesn't come directly in this time of year, but there's plenty of it."

"Do you have any other ideas?"

He shook his head. "That was it. The bed frame's made of lodgepole pine, and I have a Pendleton blanket, and I just thought maybe —"

"A Pendleton blanket?" She was already getting some ideas. The richly patterned blanket would be wonderful to design the shot with, even in black and white. And a massive bed like the one he was describing would add just the right masculine touch. Obvious as his suggestion was, it might be exactly what she needed. Tom McBride posed on a bed. The calendars would jump off the shelves.

He watched her, his gray eyes amused. "Want to go take a look?"

She considered the temptations involved. But it was the middle of the morning, for heaven's sake, and it wasn't as if they'd be alone in the house. Luann and Juanita would be around somewhere. "Okay, I'll take a look."

"How've the other sessions been coming along?" he asked as they walked side by side across the ranch yard.

"Just fine. I have one more scheduled tomorrow morning and Juanita's kids in the afternoon."

"Then I guess we need to get this accomplished today."

"I knew that, but without a solid idea about where to

do the shoot, I hated to set something up with you. I didn't want to waste your time."

"Don't worry about that." He smiled. "Out here we don't have the same fixation on time that you do back East."

"My father taught me early that time is money."

"Hmm."

"I take it you don't agree with that."

"Let's just say I grew up with a different concept. My folks used to tell us that no matter where we were going, the most important thing to take was our time."

Cleo thought about that as they walked up on the porch and Tom opened the wide front door for her. Some of her best memories of Montana were the ones in which time hadn't been a factor. The cattle drive, for example, and taking the picture of the moose. Even her own solitary ride, though it had ended so dramatically, had been free of time restraints.

And, to be totally honest with herself, the moments with Tom in the warm mineral water had completely transcended time. She wouldn't have been able to say whether they'd spent an hour together or five minutes. She only knew that the experience would be part of her memories forever.

No one was in the large living room as they walked through and headed for the polished wooden staircase leading to the second floor. A little more activity would have made Cleo feel better about this encounter, but she'd look like a scared rabbit if she backed out of going up those stairs with Tom.

"Did you slide down this banister when you were a kid?" she asked, running her hand along the smooth wood.

"Yep. Taught my sister how to do it, too. We thought nobody knew what we were up to, until Dad caught us one day and admitted he and my uncle used to slide down it all the time, and so had my grandfather. That's why it's like satin—all those little fannies sailing down from the second floor."

Cleo laughed. "What a great tradition."

"Yeah, it was."

His use of the past tense told her that he thought the tradition was over, either because he wouldn't have children or because he wasn't sure he'd keep the ranch. He should do both, she thought. Yet in order to have children, he'd have to marry someone and father them. That idea didn't sit so well with her.

After passing a sign that said Guests Prohibited Beyond This Point, she walked with him down a long hallway that seemed to carry them farther and farther from the center of the house. "Kind of secluded up here, aren't you?"

"The guests have access to just about every other square foot of the Whispering Winds. This wing I keep for myself."

So they were in a private wing of an already large house, she thought uneasily. "You know, maybe this isn't such a good—"

"Here we are." He opened the door at the end of the hall and stepped back.

Moving through the doorway, she caught her breath at the magnificence of the large room that spanned the entire south side of the house. She always noticed light first, and the sunshine coming through the bank of windows was an artist's dream. The view itself was spectacular, but the light—she lusted after this sort of luminescent glow, knowing how it could infuse her shots with magic. As the light flowed into the room unfettered by window coverings, it gently picked out the details of furnishings that suited Tom perfectly.

The bed's massive headboard and footboard dominated the room. The spread, a nubby white, was only a backdrop for a huge Pendleton blanket that might have been custom-made. Its brown and orange print was faded from years of sunlight streaming into the room. Cleo walked closer and smoothed a hand over the wool, worn soft as velvet. Decorative pillows covered in a different Pendleton fabric were tossed against the headboard, along with fluffy bed pillows encased in snowy linen.

She turned to survey the rest of the room, finding it neat without being fussy. A plush towel hung from the knob of a door that led into the master bathroom. A flannel shirt was tossed over the back of a straight-backed oak chair, and a pair of worn boots sat in a corner near an oak dresser. The dresser top served as a gallery for several framed photos, many of them sepia-toned. As she walked over to look at the pictures, she took a deep breath and realized that the room held Tom's scent. That scent was making her more than a little crazy.

"Your family?" she asked, striving for nonchalance.

"About three generations' worth."

She studied the pictures and recognized the ranch house in the background of most of them. "Tom, is there a chance you could lose this place?" She turned to find him leaning in the doorway, watching her.

He adjusted the tilt of his Stetson. "I reckon you've been talking to Juanita."

"No, I—"

"Don't bother covering up for her. It's okay. When you two became chummy, I figured she might confide a few things in you. She's been wanting a woman around to talk to. Luann isn't quite her speed."

"Okay, Juanita told me she was worried. Does she have reason to be?"

He walked into the room, his boots echoing on the hardwood floor. "Why the concern? You'll be gone soon."

She looked into his eyes and knew she'd have to be very careful in this room. It would be too easy to forget herself and her code of ethics. "You're right. It's none of my business."

"It's nice of you to be concerned," he said, his expression softening. "I guess the place found its way into your heart a little bit."

"Of course it did." *And so did you.* She tried to pretend her pulse wasn't hammering. "You have a wonderful spot here. I don't know how precarious your finances are, but if you'll let this calendar work for you, it will increase your business among single women. With you on the cover, and Jose and Jeeter inside, the ranch will look very appealing to women who have a romantic image of cowboys."

He frowned. "I'm running a guest ranch, not an escort service."

"And I'm not saying these women will expect anything different. If they do, I'm sure all of you can handle it just fine."

"Meaning?" He stood close enough to kiss her.

She trembled. "Come on, Tom. I'm sure you don't live like a monk out here."

"I don't generally get involved with guests, either."

She tried to be flip. "Then the hot tub doesn't usually come with a cowboy included?"

"Only in your case." His gaze reached into hers for a long, tense moment. "Are you sure you want that calendar picture, Cleo?"

She swallowed and stepped back. "Yes. And you're right. This is the perfect place, just as you predicted. If you're free this afternoon, I'll—"

"I'm free."

"Then I'll meet you up here at three." She edged around him, heading toward the door.

"You don't want to get your camera and start now?"

"No, I...need to clean the lens." Lame, lame, lame. But it was all she could come up with to postpone the session. She needed time to shore up her defenses before she walked back into this pressure cooker of a bedroom. "I'll see you at three."

He touched the brim of his hat. "Yes, ma'am."

12

CLEO NEEDED one more bracing, career-oriented talk with Bernie before she walked back into Tom's bedroom. She needed to remind herself of her goals, and what was best for both her and Tom. She used the ranch-house phone while everyone else was eating lunch, because for the first time in recent memory she had no appetite.

"I'm glad you called," Bernie said. "I hated to wait until I picked you up at the airport, but it seemed silly to bother you on your last two days."

"What's up?"

"You know I wasn't overjoyed at the idea of bringing your father's company in for cross-promotion, but I have to tell you, it was a smart move."

"Really?"

"Instead of just offering the calendars as a premium for buying Sphinx cosmetics, he wants to go the other way, too, and offer Sphinx cosmetics as part of the calendar package. They're coming up with a whole line of products with a Western theme to coordinate with the calendar. Now that I see old Calvin Griffin in action, I understand why he's where he is. The man's a marketing genius. Everybody involved with this project is going to make money, lots of money."

Cleo thought immediately of how that might help Tom keep the ranch. "That's good, Bernie. And the best part is, I've just about nailed my cover picture, and it's going to be hot."

"Just about? I figured you'd know who you were using by now. That Jose character wouldn't be bad, or—"

"You haven't seen the shot I want to use because I'm taking it this afternoon. I want Tom McBride for the cover, and he's agreed to let me use him if he sees the proofs first."

"Hold it. Proof approval? Who are you and what have you done with Cleo?"

"I know it's unusual for me to allow a subject to approve the proofs of a session, but—"

"Unusual? Try never in the history of your career. This makes me nervous, babe. We don't have a lot of time to jack around with this. You'll have to mail him proofs, and he'll probably be out rounding up cattle or something and not get to it for weeks, and production needs to start by—"

"Don't worry, I'm shooting thirteen cowboys, like I originally planned, so if Tom doesn't work out, we'll still have our calendar."

"Which reminds me. Should I start looking for a matron-of-honor dress?"

"I've, uh, sort of abandoned that plan for now."

"Good thing, because a wedding could really louse up the schedule for this calendar, and I'll tell you, we want to have our ducks in a row when Calvin comes to call with his Sphinx Cosmetics team."

"We'll be ready," Cleo said. "See you in two days."

TOM STOOD in front of his bedroom windows at five minutes before three. He'd cranked a couple of the windows open a few inches to let in the breeze and cool his heated body.

Right on time, Cleo stepped out of her cabin. She was hatless, and the sunlight danced like a spotlight on her jumble of blond curls. He admired the purposeful way she walked, as if she dared anyone to get in her way. He also admired her single-minded attitude and her courage in the face of adversity. They were good traits for a Montana woman to have. They were also the traits that might keep them apart.

He thought she needed more than a love of photography to keep her satisfied, but he could be wrong. What would happen between them, or not happen, was up to Cleo now. If she could maintain her professional distance throughout this photo shoot, that would be a pretty clear demonstration of her ability to put her career ahead of her emotional needs. She had a right to do that, and he'd respect her choice, but he had to know what that choice would be before he risked his heart.

He'd left strict instructions with Juanita and Jose that he was not to be disturbed, short of an emergency, until morning. They probably knew exactly what was going on, but neither of them had said a word or even lifted an eyebrow. Juanita's glance had communicated quite clearly that she thought it was about time.

Cleo had said she doubted that he lived like a monk. She might be surprised to discover he had been doing exactly that. She might be even more surprised to learn that she wasn't the only one dealing with the problem of sexual frustration.

To his amazement, he discovered he wasn't any good at casual sex anymore. Once upon a time, before Deidre, he'd cut a pretty wide swath through this valley, but marriage had shown him the joys of making love to the same woman, and he'd learned to treasure continuity. Although he mistrusted wedded bliss after the way Deidre had treated him, he wasn't ready to go back to his former sexual pursuits, either.

He was in a bind very similar to Cleo's, come to think of it.

"I'm here."

The sound of her voice skittered up his spine. He turned. "So I see."

She cleared her throat. "Well, I've been thinking about various poses, and I think we should start with—"

"I think we should start with closing the door."

She glanced around at the open doorway. "Oh, I don't think that's necessary, do you?"

"It's absolutely necessary. It isn't logical, considering that I may end up on a calendar the world is going to see, but I'll be damned if the photo session is going to be a public one."

"All right." She closed the door.

Instantly the atmosphere in the room intensified. His heart began chugging along like a freight train as he looked at her across the broad expanse of mattress separating them.

"I'd like you to sit on the bed," she said. "The side closest to the windows, so I can get that light falling on your face."

"Okay." He sat down and propped his hands behind him. "Now what?"

She licked her lips and took the lens cap off her camera. "Let me get a reading, here."

He looked straight into the lens as she crouched and pointed it at him.

"Nice," she said. "The light's perfect. Nudge your hat back a little."

He used his thumb to do what she asked, but he kept his gaze trained on that lens, because he knew she was looking into it and that was the only way to maintain eye contact with her.

"For someone who didn't want his picture taken, you seem pretty relaxed."

"Maybe because I finally got a few things straight, and I know what I want out of this."

She swallowed and clicked the shutter a couple of times. "Good. I talked to my assistant at noon, and we have some exciting cross-promotion lined up for the calendar." She moved a few steps and clicked the shutter again. She was going through the motions, but there was no style, no flair. "Bernie predicted that anyone connected with this project will make good money. That should be welcome news for you."

"That's assuming you'll be able to take a decent picture this afternoon."

"What?" She brought the camera down and stared at him.

"All this talk about cross-promotions and money isn't very sexy, and it isn't your usual approach, judging from what I've seen. You're holding back, Cleo."

"I just need to get warmed up!"

He spoke low and easy. "Can I help?"

"No! I mean..." She looked confused. Then she hung the camera from her neck and ran her fingers through her hair. "You're right. I'm tense. I've never shot a guy

I...have feelings for. This is more awkward than I thought it would be."

"Maybe I can help, after all." He began unbuttoning his shirt.

"Wait!"

He almost smiled at the panic in her voice. He paused and lifted an eyebrow.

"Take...take off your boots. That's it. The rancher at the end of the day sitting on the edge of his bed, taking off his boots. I like that."

"All right." He had the first boot off and was about to drop it to floor.

"Look at me," she commanded, crouching in front of him.

He did, although he deliberately didn't put a whole lot of expression into it. With her scent tantalizing him and her body almost within reach, keeping cool wasn't easy, but he'd do it. She was going to have to work to get what she wanted out of him.

She took the picture, but he could tell from her frown that she wasn't satisfied. "Okay, the other boot. Easy. Take it off slow. There. Look at me again. That's better."

Damn, but her voice was having an effect on him. He felt some heat transfer with that shot.

She stood and paced in front of him. "Let me think for a minute."

"You didn't have to think when you were shooting Jeeter."

"Don't you suppose I know that?" Her blue eyes flashed. "Jeeter was just another calendar page, but this...this has to be special."

"Then you'll have to go for it, Cleo," he said softly.

She stood in front of him, her gaze troubled, her body trembling slightly.

He lowered his voice another notch. "Unless you want to forget the calendar shot and just have a good time."

Her jaw clenched. "No, by God, we're going to do this. Take off your shirt."

He took his time unsnapping the cuffs and pulling the tail from the waistband of his jeans while he stared into the camera lens. He could hear the pattern of her breathing change when he finally took off the shirt and tossed it on the floor.

"Lean back on your elbows." Her tone was uneven, but there was a thread of determination running through it.

He gazed into the camera. "Aren't you going to tell me how good I look without a shirt?"

She swore softly, and he smiled. Click, click, click went the shutter as she moved closer, leaning over him slightly. "Undo the belt."

He was getting hard. Unhooking the belt buckle made him painfully aware of just how aroused he was.

"The top button." She clicked the shutter furiously now.

"I want you, Cleo."

"Don't tell me that." Her chest was heaving as she changed her camera angle. "Next button."

He complied, very slowly. "You can see how much I want you. Let me strip you naked and make love to you on this blanket."

"Stop it!" She took two more frames.

"Let me show you all the ways I can touch you, all the ways I can give you pleasure."

"No." She was breathing hard and kept shooting.

"I want to see the look on your face when I'm deep inside you."

"What are you doing?" she cried, the camera clutched in her shaking hands as she battled for control.

He sat up slowly, tossed his hat aside and took the camera from her unresisting fingers. "Trying to make you see," he murmured, lifting the strap over her head and laying the camera on the bedside table. "Did you get what you wanted?"

Her eyes were moist, her words choked. "I don't know."

"I believe you really don't." He drew her gently down and guided her back onto the blanket. "Let's see if maybe this could be it." He started on the buttons of her shirt.

"I can't." Her hair in disarray against the bold patterned wool, she gazed at him. "I can't, Tom." Yet she made no move to stop him.

"Yes, you can." He leaned down and kissed the soft skin of her throat as he continued to undress her.

"I've never...let one of my subjects..."

"This time you will." He worked her out of her clothes, caressing her firm breasts, her narrow waist, her silken thighs. She trembled and moaned beneath his touch, thrashing her head from side to side as if to deny what was happening, but she still didn't stop him.

Finally he lifted her more fully onto the bed and admired the contrast of her white skin against the bold colors of the blanket. "Perfect."

"No, Tom." She struggled for breath. "Really. We can't do this. We—"

He silenced her with a deep kiss that left her vibrating in his arms.

"But I don't want to," she wailed when her mouth was free again.

"Is that right?" he murmured against her breast.

With a downward stroke of his hand he sought the fevered dampness between her thighs. "I think you have a credibility problem, sweetheart."

"I'm so afraid that I'll..." She gasped as he probed deep.

"That you'll find out you're human? That a man can make you lose control of that famous discipline?"

"Yes!"

"That's why I'm here." He lifted his head to gaze into her eyes. "I need to see that happen."

"You planned this all along," she whispered.

"I wanted this all along. But I won't force you." He teased her lightly with his fingers. "Tell me to stop and I'll stop."

"St..."

He paused, his heartbeat thudding in his ears as he waited.

"Stay," she murmured at last, the word ending on a sigh. "Please stay. Love me until I can't think anymore."

Joy surged through him as he smiled tenderly down at her. "Yes, ma'am. I'd be happy to."

THE TOUCH OF HIS HANDS and mouth on her body swept away most of her control. The rest of it disappeared when he shucked his jeans and rolled a condom over his sizable erection.

"Now," she said, panting, needing him to fill the aching void within her. "Now, Tom."

"Yes, now."

She gazed upon the rugged beauty of him as he moved over her, and her throat tightened with the sudden urge to cry. She reached up to cup his face in both hands, to memorize the way he was looking at her with a perfect mix of tenderness and passion. And she knew she'd never capture that look with a camera.

He turned his head to kiss her palm that rested against his cheek. Then he looked down at her again. "The night in the hot tub was just fooling around," he murmured, stroking her with the tip of his shaft against her sensitive folds. "I'm through fooling around, Cleo."

"I'm not sure...what you mean." Her voice quivered.

"When we're finished here, you will be." He slid his hands beneath her bottom, lifting her to meet him as he pushed in deep.

"*Oh.*" The cry rushed from her, propelled by a feeling of completeness she'd never known. He filled her, blotting out everything but the sensation of joining with her destiny.

"Ah, Cleo." He smiled gently as he drew back and completed the miracle once again.

"Tom," she said, gasping. "Tom, I—" Words failed her.

"Just enjoy, sweetheart." He moved slowly within her, setting off ripples of pleasure with every thrust. "Life doesn't give us times like this too often."

She'd always considered sex a frantic, sometimes confusing business. Tom was not the least bit confused. He knew exactly what he was doing, and what he was doing was incredible. Tension drained from all parts of her body to settle in one spot, and there he lavished all his attention. Marveling at the perfection of each movement, Cleo surrendered the last of her discipline, the last of her control, for the first time in her life.

"Now you're starting to give in to it," he murmured. "Just relax. We're going to take this slow and make it last."

For the first time she didn't question who was in command. He was solidly in charge, guiding her through a foreign and exciting land, one she'd never allowed herself to travel before, never trusted a man to navigate for her. Oh, she'd taken her pleasure, but always on her own terms, always with restraint.

Restraint slipped away. She arched against him, letting him know how she craved what he was giving her, shameless in her vulnerability.

"Yes, my darling. Yes," he whispered. Easing her bottom down to the blanket again, he braced his hands on either side of her head without breaking his steady rhythm. But his angle changed. The light sprinkle of hair that curled over his chest tickled her breasts as he created a new kind of friction with each thrust.

She gazed into his eyes, soft as rain clouds, yet she sensed the storm he kept in check while he led her through a garden of delights, building the tension within her. When he quickened the rhythm, she was helpless in his arms, swirling rapidly in an exotic river filled with frothy rapids and bright flowers. The waterfall rushed to meet her, wringing a cry from her lips as she tumbled over it.

He slowed the tempo, absorbed her convulsions against his body, and kept moving. Speechless, sated with the force of her climax, she looked at him in wonder.

His smile made her heart tremble. "I think that's what you wanted," he said gently as he eased back and forth, maintaining the thread of tension.

She thought so, too, but couldn't manage a single word.

"But there's even more." He wrapped his arms around her, snugged in tight and rolled to his back, bringing her with him.

Limp and languid though she was, she still found herself drawing her knees up on either side of his hips and bracing her hands beside his shoulders so that she could keep that delicious momentum going.

Gradually she found her capacity for speech return. Hair falling around her face, she met his gaze as she moved sensuously and deliberately toward another climax. "I feel wanton," she murmured. She felt far more than that, but lacked the courage to say it.

"That's the idea." He cupped her swaying breasts in both hands.

She loved the way he was touching her breasts, and the glow in his eyes as he looked at her naked body in the afternoon light. "But I've never...felt this way." *In love.*

"Then it's time you did. You... Mmm." He closed his eyes and clenched his jaw. "Wow. You nearly made me...oh, Cleo, take it easy."

"You put me on top, cowboy. Take the consequences."

He grasped her hips. "I can put you back on the bottom again, too. You're dealing with a steer wrestler."

"Don't." She leaned down and brushed her lips against his. "Let me take you with me this time."

He kept her close with a hand behind her head. "Your lips are so sweet," he said, urging her down to him. "Kiss me again. And make it count."

She did, telling him with the language of her lips and tongue what she dared not say out loud. His grip tightened on her bottom and his upward thrusts became more powerful. She took his moan of completion into her mouth as an answering explosion rocked her body. It was perfect. All of it. She'd broken her cardinal rule, and nothing had ever felt so right before.

ALL THE JANGLE of nerves that had kept Cleo from sleeping for years had quieted, and she dozed beside Tom as they lay sprawled on the patterned blanket. At last, the cool breeze from the window woke her. The wonderful light that had seduced her into coming into this bedroom was nearly gone.

She slipped out of bed without waking Tom and walked over to gaze at the ranch in the glow of late afternoon. The sound of a dog barking drew her gaze to the woods, where a group of riders came out of the trees headed for the corral. She stepped away from the window, although she was certain no one could see her from this distance.

Instead, she turned back to the bed and saw how the last light of day spilled across it, caressing the magnificent body of the cowboy sprawled there on his stomach, one arm flung out as if reaching for her.

She crept to the bedside table and picked up her camera. Five frames left on the roll. She sighted through the lens, moved a fraction and sighted again. In the orange light his sculpted body looked like bronze. The patterned blanket provided the perfect backdrop, and for once she wished she had a color roll. She'd love to be able to capture the rosy flush of his skin and the rich brown of his hair tipped with sunlight.

She took one shot, and another. Excitement rose within her. The composition, the light, the subject were all perfect. She moved to another vantage point and took a third shot. And a fourth. If what she saw through the viewfinder was what came out on film, these could be the best photos of her career.

On the fifth snap of the shutter, Tom's eyes opened.

"What are you doing?"

"Taking your picture."

The haze of sleep cleared from his eyes as he propped himself on one elbow. "Do you develop your own film?"

"No. I have a special lab that—"

"I guess that settles the question of whether I'll be in your calendar."

Uneasiness gripped her heart. "It does?"

"Sexy pictures are one thing. Nude pictures are a whole other subject."

"I wouldn't use these for the calendar!" No, she'd pictured putting them in an art show in the middle of Manhattan, and blowing them up to poster size.

"I don't care. My bare ass isn't going through some photo lab. You'll have to destroy the film."

13

"No! I won't destroy this film." Cleo held the camera to her chest, as if he might wrench it away from her.

Tom sighed and moved over to sit on the edge of the bed. This wasn't the mood he'd hoped to set when they awoke from the best lovemaking he'd ever experienced, and he hoped the best she'd ever known, too. She looked so damn good standing there, the light outlining her body like those auras he'd read about. "What did you plan to do with the pictures?"

She flushed, which made her look even more appealing. "Nothing without your permission, of course."

"And what did you plan to ask my permission for?"

"Nobody would recognize you. Your face was in shadow."

He saw red. "You wanted to *show* them to someone?"

"Tom, if I got what I think I did, they're wonderful. They're not just pictures, they're art. In a gallery, they could—"

"A *gallery?*" He came off the bed and started toward her.

"Don't yell," she said, backing away from him. "Somebody will hear you."

"I can yell if I damn well want to in my own house! And I want to!" He advanced on her. "Because that may be the only way you understand that my naked butt is never, and I mean never, going to be hanging in some gallery in New York City, or any other place on this planet! Got that?"

"Don't be so provincial." She backed up until she reached the oak chair, which halted her escape.

"I will be, because I am. I'm from rural Montana, lady, not the big city, and out here we don't go in for nude art, especially yours truly."

"Your name wouldn't be on it or anything. That's only for the calendar pictures, so they know the men are real. This is more like a fantasy, with the way the light fell, and I blurred the focus just slightly. It could very well be the best thing I've ever done. It could win awards."

He stared at her. "Let me get this straight. You objected to sleeping with me if you planned to put my picture in your calendar, but you don't mind sleeping with me and then parading my slightly blurred body all over New York?"

"That's right! Because the calendars are deliberately provocative, and the men are completely identified, so I have to make sure everyone knows I don't sleep with my subjects. That would be extremely unprofessional, and unfair to them, as well. In photography circles I would be called an artistic slut, with a great deal of justification."

"But sleeping with someone, taking his picture afterward and making it into an art print wouldn't be unprofessional?"

"No, it wouldn't, because the shots I took of you aren't provocative."

"Oh, no?" He glowered at her. "I have no clothes on, and I'm sprawled on a bed. That's pretty damn provocative, if you ask me."

"They're subtly sensuous, not overtly arousing, because I took them with tenderness and an eye for beauty."

He nearly choked. "Beauty?"

"Yes, beauty. Seeing you there, lying in that special shaft of light, with your hair all tousled, and shadows made by the muscles of your back, and your gentle hands spread out on the blanket..." She shrugged, making her breasts quiver. "The artist in me had to take those pictures. They weren't taken for gain, they were taken for love, and..." She glanced away. "What's the use? You don't understand me, anyway."

His heart squeezed. "I think I just understood some of it," he murmured, tilting her chin back around. "Come here a minute." He took her by the shoulders and turned her so he could slide onto the chair and ease her onto his lap. The pictures had been taken with love, she'd said. He'd gained more ground than he'd even hoped for.

She nestled against his shoulder, but she kept a firm hand on her camera. "Please don't ask me to destroy that film. You have every right to, of course. I said I wouldn't do it, but that was just bravado. I'd have to if you insisted, because I couldn't even develop the film without your consent."

"I told you from the beginning that I'm a private man. What we just shared is private." He breathed in the womanly scent of her and stroked her hair, working through the little tangles he'd helped create.

"I know. But you really won't be recognized. Besides, the lab doesn't pay attention to what it processes. It has a lot of clients who specialize in nude art, and I'm sure the people there have seen more naked bodies than a hospital staff. They're immune by now."

He was far from immune to one particular naked body. In fact, she was getting further with her argument by sitting on his lap than she had with all her logical reasoning. "Let me think about it," he said, knowing he probably wouldn't get much thinking done in this position, skin to skin with the sexiest woman he'd ever met. "Since you don't sleep with your calendar subjects, are you going to forget about using me for the cover?"

"Well, I violated my rule."

And how, he thought, trailing a finger down the slope of her breast and circling her nipple. It tightened in response. "Since it's your rule, I guess you have to decide what to do about it."

"Even if I want to use you in the calendar, you might decide against it when I send you the proofs."

"The proofs with my bare-butt shots included, I suppose." He teased the other nipple to erectness. A similar stiffening behavior was going on in his lap.

"Yes."

"But if I said the word, you'd take the film out and give it to me now?"

She stirred in his arms and sat up a little straighter. Her thighs rubbed sweetly against his erection.

"I'll give it to you now."

He wished she wasn't talking about film.

Apparently, she was. She opened the camera and took out the finished roll. "I'll leave it on your bedside table until tomorrow, so you have complete control over what happens to it." She stood, went to the bed and put the film on the table.

"Cleo, don't go yet. We—"

She set down the camera, opened the drawer and pulled out a condom. "Oh, I'm not leaving yet," she said, walking back to him with a decided sway to her hips. "The way I look at it, I might as well be hanged for a sheep as a lamb." Her gaze drifted to his lap. "And from the looks of things, you're ready to continue aiding my fall from grace."

He eyed the condom as she took it out of the package. "Do you have more film?"

"I always have more film. Want some kinky shots to remember me by?"

"God, no. I want you to promise me you won't reload that damn camera again."

"I promise." She dropped to her knees in front of him and rolled the condom over his hardened shaft. Standing again, she grasped the back of the chair and straddled both it and him. "I'll just concentrate on reloading you." With a smooth downward movement, she welcomed him back to paradise.

CLEO DECIDED she must be making up for lost time. Apparently Tom was, too. They couldn't seem to get enough of each other. Somewhere near midnight they pulled on enough clothes to cover the essentials and raided the refrigerator in Juanita's spotless kitchen. Afterward they tried to clean up the evidence.

"She'll still know we were here," Tom said after they gave the counter one last swipe and headed back upstairs.

"It's okay. I have kitchen privileges."

He slung an arm around her shoulders. "Do you realize that no one else has ever wangled that kind of treatment from Juanita?"

"She likes my calendars."

He pulled her over for a kiss as they walked down the hall toward his bedroom. "She likes you."

She savored the taste of him, flavored now with the roast beef and cheese sandwiches they'd just finished. "I like her, too. I like her coffee almost as much as I do her, and that's saying a lot. I'm going to miss both of them." She could talk about missing Juanita. What she couldn't talk about, couldn't even think about, was missing Tom.

He guided her through the door and closed it tight before turning to her. "Cleo..."

She saw in his eyes what was coming next. She shook her head. "I can't do that to you."

"Do what?"

"Involve you with a New York woman again. Make you suffer going to the city because I couldn't always come out here. And there's something else. You're going to have children someday. You'll find the right woman and have those kids, because otherwise there won't be a McBride to take over the ranch." She waved a hand toward the photos on his dresser. "This place is full of continuity. You deserve to find someone who can help you create the next generation."

His gaze searched hers.

She felt her womb tighten and told herself it was mere sexual desire, not some primitive mating instinct. "Don't look at me like that. I'm not the maternal type."

"Aren't you?" Slipping the buttons free on her blouse, he cradled her breast and looked into her eyes as he stroked his thumb across her nipple.

In spite of herself, she pictured a tiny mouth there, seeking nourishment. A baby with Tom's eyes and her hair. Her voice grew husky. "You're the sort of man who would make any woman think of children, whether she wants to or not."

"That's not true." He cupped her bottom and pulled her against his erection. "But you're thinking of it."

Yes, she was. His arousal carried a different message this time, created a different sort of ache deep within her. "That's only because we've spent the past few hours in the activity that can result in babies, and now I brought up the subject. It's only natural that I'm...aware of...of..." She became lost in the depths of his gaze.

His tone was low and intense. "After what happened, I never thought I'd want to make a woman pregnant again."

She swallowed. The ache within her threatened to overpower everything.

He stroked her belly as he looked deep into her eyes. "It seems I was wrong."

Heat rushed through her, and she was suddenly desperate for his solid fullness deep inside her—all of him loving her, with no barriers. She reached for the snap on his jeans. "Make love to me."

They managed to get as far as the edge of the bed. He leaned her back across the mattress, her feet still on the floor as he shoved her slacks down. Insanity claimed her as she released him from his jeans and opened her thighs.

"Wait. We need—"

"No." She kicked the slacks free and wrapped her legs around his hips.

"Just for...a minute," he gasped. "Just until..."

She moaned aloud as he plunged inside her. In a few quick strokes she exploded.

"Cleo, I can't...stop." He buried himself inside her trembling body with a guttural cry of surrender.

"I SHOULDN'T HAVE done that." He'd refastened his jeans and now stood in front of the windows looking into the night.

"It takes two to be stupid." Cleo pulled on her clothes. "You tried to stop me from behaving like a mare in season. I wouldn't let you." Her feelings were so jumbled, she couldn't make sense of anything. She'd loved what had just happened, yet it could ruin both their lives. She should be horrified, when instead she was filled with joy.

"I helped bring you into season," he said, "if you want to use that comparison. I saw that look in your eyes and I encouraged you."

"Don't worry," she said, coming over to put a hand on his arm. "One wild moment doesn't usually result in...an accident."

He turned and clasped his hands around her upper arms. "You're whistling in the dark, Cleo." His eyes were stormy. "You opened to me the way a flower opens for a bee, and you know it."

She did know it. Until now, all they'd done was make love. But this...this was mating. Still, the law of averages was on their side. She'd known couples who'd had unprotected sex for years and had never conceived the child they wanted. "You're a romantic," she said, smiling at him. "And you're also paranoid, which is understandable. We'll be fine."

His grip tightened. "And what if you're carrying our child?"

That would be a disaster, she thought, although she couldn't help continuing to smile at him. She was turning into a brainless twit who could only smile despite impending ruin. "I promise you that I won't do what Deidre did."

"Why not?"

Because I love you. But she didn't say those words. If she did, he might follow her to New York, and neglect the ranch again, as he probably had when Deidre was a part of his life. "Because you have rights, too," she said. "Rights that Deidre ignored. I would have the baby and turn the child immediately over to you. I can't think of a better place to grow up than the Whispering Winds, and Juanita would take...really good care of..." She cleared the lump from her throat. "This is silly. I'm sure I'm not pregnant."

He drew her close and caressed her cheek. "I wouldn't just want the baby. I'd want you."

"I know." She gazed up at him. "But I'm the wrong woman."

"I don't think so." His kiss was desperate.

She couldn't help responding, because she was feeling pretty desperate, herself. But she had to get out of that room before she started agreeing to things that would be a mistake for both of them. With an effort she pulled away.

"I'm going back to my cabin."

"I'll walk you there."

"No. If you do, I'll want you to come in, and we'll just start all over again."

"So what? I promise we'll use protection." He reached for her.

She stepped back, away from the temptation of his strong arms. "That's the problem. I liked it too much without."

With a groan he moved quickly and hauled her back against him. "You belong with me, Cleo. Stop fighting it and—"

"And give up everything I've worked so hard for?" She looked into his beloved face, knowing this decision was as important for him as for her. "No. Let me go, Tom. Let me go so I can find the strength to walk away from you. You and this ranch have cast a spell over me. It's a glorious spell, but it's not what I want for the rest of my life. Let me go."

She looked away from the anguish in his eyes as he loosened his hold on her and stepped back. Then she walked over and picked up her camera bag. Not trusting herself to say anything more, she started from the room.

"Take the film."

She glanced back at him.

"You can have it. Develop the damn pictures and use them any way you want. At least that's one way I can stay in your life."

Swallowing back the tears, she went to the bedside table and picked up the roll of film. Now she had everything she wanted. Sure she did. "Thanks," she whispered, and walked out the door.

HE WATCHED HER walk across the yard back to her cabin, watched until she was safely inside the door. Well, at least he hadn't groveled. At least she had no idea how much he needed her at this very moment. Several times tonight he'd thought about telling her the latest news. Now he was glad he hadn't.

His mother's voice on the phone this morning had been teary. She'd found some papers his father had hidden, and in his mental deterioration, probably forgotten. If Tom had been paying more attention to such things instead of being so wrapped up in Deidre, and later in her secret abortion and the divorce, he might have been more aware of his father's activities.

But he'd left that angle to his dad, not wanting to admit that his father was losing his grip on reality and couldn't be trusted to handle the ranch finances. Now here was another banknote, another lien on the Whispering Winds. A balloon payment was due in two weeks, and if it wasn't paid, the ranch would be lost.

He'd had some crazy idea that with Cleo by his side he'd be able to stave off the inevitable. And even if he lost the ranch, having Cleo would make life seem worth living. But she didn't want to be a Montana rancher's wife. She'd made that perfectly clear.

If she turned out to be pregnant, and he had a gut feeling she was, she'd send the baby to him to raise, because she was a woman of her word. He'd go along with that, no matter what sacrifices he had to make in the process. But chances were, that kid wouldn't be raised, as she'd so lovingly described, on the Whispering Winds.

CLEO KEPT her appointment with the thirteenth cowboy the next morning as a safety measure. Considering her mental state when she'd been snapping those pictures of Tom, she didn't know if she'd have anything usable.

The pictures she'd taken after they'd made love were a different story. But the calendar shots might be trash.

After her sleepless night she was running on pure adrenaline as she drove the replacement convertible the rental agency had delivered. She'd discovered a wooded area near a picnic grounds and had suggested meeting Jake there. The pose she had in mind involved him leaning against a ponderosa pine she'd discovered that already had a heart and initials carved into it. Perfect for February. Even if the shots of Tom worked, she might suggest to Bernie that they publish a thirteen-month calendar that began in December, so she could use everyone, including Jake.

She pulled into the parking area and cut the engine. Her hand went to her stomach, as it had been doing many times in the past few hours. Of course she wasn't pregnant. She just needed to get away from Tom, out of Montana, and these crazy notions would disappear. She didn't even want to think of how she'd tell her father such a thing. But that wouldn't be necessary because she wasn't carrying Tom's child.

Jake hadn't arrived, so she got out and walked the short distance to the tree she'd found. The scent of warm pine needles reminded her of the night in the hot tub. She put a hand on the tree's rough bark and looked up into branches that climbed fifty feet into the air. Then she traced the heart carved into the side of the tree, and the crude initials. B.R. + D.S. Tears filled her eyes as she pictured the earnest young lovers eager to tell the world of their bond.

It was a simple and elegant process. You found someone, fell in love and promised to cherish them forever. You didn't audition candidates in front of your camera.

And you didn't, she realized now, meet on alternate weekends for sex. She'd never be able to stand so much time away from a man like Tom. More and more, she was realizing that she wouldn't get married at all. As he'd said, she wasn't capable of doing something half-way.

Jake arrived in his gleaming black pickup. He had a lot of swagger to him as he climbed down and walked toward her. She often looked for swagger, because it meant the subjects already knew how to project their sexuality.

He touched the brim of his white straw cowboy hat. "You're looking fine, ma'am."

"Thank you. You, too." And he did, she thought. Tight jeans, polished boots, a muscle shirt and the muscles to go with it. Intense black eyes and raven hair worn just a little long. Women would go wild looking at him next February. But she didn't feel a thing.

She'd work into it, she told herself. That little twinge of sexual excitement she always felt at the beginning of a shoot was just slightly late this time. "As I told you, I want to use this tree over here." She walked back toward the ponderosa and he followed her.

Jake chuckled. "I know the ol' boy who carved those initials."

"You do?"

"Yeah. Went to high school with him. Last I heard, he and Donna had about five kids."

Cleo touched her stomach again. "Really? How about you? Do you have any children?"

"No, ma'am! Don't know if I ever want any. Kids are a lot of trouble."

"And what does your girlfriend think of that?"

He glanced at her. "To be honest, Suzanne and I broke up over it. She's married now, and already has a baby on the way."

"Oh." She felt rotten for probing into his personal life. "I'm sorry. I shouldn't have asked."

He gave her a lazy grin. "Why not? That's what most women do when they're trying to find out if a guy's available, and that's exactly what I am. How about you? Somebody special in your life?"

Here he was, she thought. The perfect candidate to fall in with her husband-hunting plan. He was about her age, maybe a couple of years younger. Wanted a carefree existence. Looked great in jeans, and probably knew his way around a bedroom. He'd probably love the idea of a once-in-a-while wife. Too bad the concept didn't appeal to her at all anymore.

"Looks like I asked too personal a question, myself," he said. "Sorry."

"No, it's not too personal." She tried to push Tom out of her mind. She couldn't do it. "Yes, there is someone."

"I wondered. There's that certain glow women get when they're either in love or feverish. I'm glad you're not sick."

"Not sick," she said. "Just crazy. Come on, let's get the shots taken."

"I'm ready."

She instructed him to lean a shoulder and hip against the tree. Then she got below him, shooting upward to emphasize his crotch and the strong jut of the tree. It was an extremely sexual angle. Normally, she'd be reacting to the suggestive nature of the pose, but she might as well have been taking a photo of a haystack.

"You have a great physique," she said, but instead of

the husky tone she normally used to work her men into a lather, the comment came out sounding like a clinical evaluation.

"Thanks."

She cursed to herself. She had to get into the mood somehow, and she didn't have all day to do it. "Tell me what you like best about a woman's body," she said.

He laughed. "Is this supposed to be X-rated or the family channel?"

"Make it sexy. That's what we're here for, to capture a little lust."

"Okay. Then I'd have to say a woman's breasts are my favorite. I love touching them, holding them, kissing them, especially if she really likes that, too." His eyes grew smoky with desire. "And her nipples, the way they get hard when I run my tongue around them. I love doing that when I'm inside her, and she's all shivery, anyway." The tight fit of his jeans made his arousal obvious.

Cleo took advantage of the moment he'd created to snap frame after frame, but she'd lost the instinct that had always guided her trigger finger. Although he was totally into the mood, she wasn't. She felt no connection with his fantasy because...he wasn't Tom. When the truth hit her, she almost dropped the camera.

She surged right into denial, blaming exhaustion, Jake's tone of voice, the setting, for her lack of involvement in this shoot. But in her heart, as she clicked the shutter furiously, she knew that what she'd feared the most had indeed happened. She'd broken her rule, interrupted the flow of the creative river she'd been gliding down with such success. She'd lost the magic touch for getting the shots that had made her famous. And she was never getting it back.

14

A SIXTH SENSE made Tom take a stroll on the front porch just when Cleo drove away from the ranch to shoot her thirteenth cowboy. His gut tightened, knowing the way she normally conducted those sessions. He knew that her photo shoot this morning wouldn't end up like last night's, yet he still didn't want her pointing that camera at some cowboy on the make. He didn't want her using that sultry tone of voice that made men gaze at her with lust.

But it was her job. She'd go on doing it, whether he wanted her to or not. He might as well concentrate on something productive, like trying to negotiate more time on the balloon payment. With a sigh he walked into the house and headed for his office.

By noon he'd talked to enough self-important bank officials to last him a lifetime. He went into the dining room, hoping Cleo might have decided to eat with everyone else for a change, but she wasn't there. He spoke to several of the guests, managing to laugh and talk like a normal human being even though he felt as if somebody had hollowed him out and left only the shell.

Juanita passed by with a heaping bowl of potato salad and stopped to glance over her shoulder at him. "She's taking pictures of Rosa and Peter at two in the barn, in case you'd like to know."

"Thanks." He figured Juanita could see past the front

he was putting on for the guests to the agony inside his heart. The threat of losing the ranch was bad enough. The threat of losing Cleo, too, had nearly crippled him.

"Want to sit down and have some lunch?" Juanita asked.

He shook his head.

"Make her stay, Tom."

He forced a smile. "Don't think I can."

Juanita frowned. "Try harder." Then she continued serving the guests.

He would try harder, if he only knew what might work. But he'd given her his best last night, and it hadn't been enough. Stopping to speak to a few more guests on his way out, he left the dining room. By this time tomorrow, she'd be gone. He couldn't accept it, but he didn't know how to keep it from happening.

Going out to the corral, he threw a saddle on Red and headed out, letting the big horse run as long as the terrain allowed. He rode hard, but the peace he usually found on the back of a horse wouldn't come. Finally he turned Red's nose for home, and as the ranch came into view, he saw her drive the convertible in and park it beside her cabin. He pulled his horse to a halt and leaned on the saddle horn to watch as she climbed out and went inside.

The connection between them tugged at his insides with the strength of a steer on the end of a rope. As he nudged Red into motion again, he wondered if he'd still feel that tug when she was two thousand miles away. From the power of it, he imagined he would. But she didn't want him in New York, either. She'd also made that clear.

He took his time getting back to the corral and unsaddling his horse. He didn't want to arrive at the barn before she'd had a chance to get completely involved taking pictures of the kids. But he had to see her, had to talk with her at least once more, and this might be his only chance.

The sound of childish laughter echoed inside the barn as he drew near, and he smiled. For one brief moment he allowed himself the fantasy that Cleo was in the barn taking pictures of their children, but he couldn't dwell on the fantasy too long, not when it had such a slim chance of coming true.

Juanita glanced at him when he appeared in the open barn door, but Cleo was oblivious.

"That was a *wonderful* somersault, Peter," she said. "Do another one."

"Wanna see my cartwheel?" asked Rosa, jumping up and down in the mounds of hay Cleo had spread out for them.

"You bet." Cleo dropped to one knee, clicking away as Peter tumbled in the hay. He came up grinning, pieces of hay stuck in his dark curls. "Look this way, Peter. That's good. Do you have a teddy bear?"

Peter nodded. "Freddy the Teddy."

"How big is Freddy?"

Peter raised his hands over his head as Cleo kept the camera shutter busy.

"Here goes!" shouted Rosa.

Cleo swung her attention to Rosa's earnest attempts at a cartwheel. "That's so good," she said. "I'll bet you're going to be in the Olympics someday."

"I am," said Rosa, and flung herself over again.

Tom couldn't resist coming closer. He crouched next

to Juanita, who was sitting on a bale of hay, her face glowing with pride.

She leaned over and murmured in his ear. "Look how she is with them."

Oh, he was looking, all right. In between shots she'd call them over and pick hay out of their hair, running her fingers through their soft locks. Her touch lingered as she brushed a speck from Rosa's shirt, or refastened a button on Peter's overalls. He couldn't see her face, but he could hear the smile in her voice every time she spoke to them. She was entranced with these two children, and they'd fallen head over heels in love with her.

Judging from the unbearable pain in his heart, so had he.

He sat back on his heels and watched with bittersweet delight as the session continued. She was a natural with those kids, but he wasn't surprised. She might be, though.

"That's it," she said finally. "Film's all gone."

"Now you do one," Rosa said. "You promised."

"So I did." She set her camera down, walked over to the bed of hay they'd constructed and executed a decent cartwheel. "Ta-da!" She threw her arms up and back in a classic gymnast pose.

"Yeah!" Rosa clapped wildly and Peter grinned.

Cleo laughed and turned toward the bale of hay where Juanita was sitting. "Well, lady, I—" She caught sight of Tom for the first time. Her smile faded. "Hi. Didn't know you were there."

He stood. "I hope you don't mind."

"No, of course not." She ran her fingers through her hair and glanced away. "After all, it's your ranch."

Juanita gave him a sharp nudge in the ribs and angled her head in Cleo's direction. Then she hurried over to take each of her children by the hand. "Time for that homemade strawberry ice cream I promised you," she said.

"Yummy!" Rosa said. "Come on, Cleo. Ice cream!"

"Sounds great." Cleo tucked her camera in her bag and swung it to her shoulder.

"Uh, Cleo, could I talk to you a minute?" Tom asked, stepping closer to her.

She glanced toward the doorway as Juanita hustled the kids outside. "Okay." Her gaze returned to his. "But I don't think—"

His arms went around her and his mouth came down on hers before he even realized what he was doing.

She struggled at first, but not for long. He slid the camera strap from her shoulder and lowered the case gently to the ground as he tapped into her heat. Soon the resistance went out of her and she molded herself against him. Then, with an endearing little whimper, she opened her mouth for his tongue.

He longed to keep kissing her right through tomorrow, but that wasn't exactly a realistic plan. With great reluctance he lifted his mouth a fraction from hers. "Nice cartwheel."

"I thought you wanted to talk," she murmured.

"I thought I did, too." He ran his tongue over her lower lip. "God, you taste good."

"Tom, this is only going to make it harder."

As her comment sank in, he began to laugh. "It already has." He pressed her against his groin. "As I'm sure you can tell."

She shook her head and smiled. "Cowboys. Gotta love 'em."

"I'm glad you think so. And I have a much better treat in mind than strawberry ice cream."

"No." She pushed gently on his chest.

He let her go. "You're not leaving until tomorrow."

"Actually, I'm leaving in an hour. I've decided to spend my last night in Bozeman."

Pain sliced him to ribbons. "Don't."

She gazed at him, her blue eyes cloudy with unhappiness. "I can't risk another night here. I'm losing myself on this ranch."

"Or finding yourself."

"You don't understand." She combed her hair back with trembling fingers. "I'm Cleo Griffin, the woman who takes sizzling photos of men. That's the niche I've carved out for myself, and there aren't that many niches available, believe me."

"I've never asked you to stop doing that." He didn't like it, but he knew better than to ask her to give it up.

"I know you haven't." Her smile was sad. "That would have been easy. I could have laughed in your face and refused to abandon my career."

"Don't end what we have, Cleo." The tightness in his chest threatened to turn into full-fledged panic. She couldn't be leaving in an hour. Less than an hour now. "We can work something out, something that's good for both of us. Let's try at least."

She shook her head. "I came here on a manhunting expedition. I wanted the calendar subjects, of course, but I also wanted a man who would...give me what I need. And the joke is, I found him."

"I have a feeling I won't find this very funny."

"It is funny, if you just keep your perspective. I went out on a shoot this morning."

"I know."

"I've lost the ability to shoot sexy pictures, Tom."

He was ashamed of the selfish joy he found in that fact. "What happened?"

"It was pretty horrible, actually. Here was this gorgeous hunk of a cowboy, Jake Collins."

"I know Jake." And he was damn glad he hadn't realized who her thirteenth cowboy was. Jake was eligible, and he had a hell of a reputation for pleasing women.

"I tried to get into the mood, to create that chemistry that makes my calendar shots special." She gazed at him. "All I could think about was you."

Damn, he loved hearing that, but he shouldn't love it. She was telling him she might have just committed career suicide. That was the term Deidre had used to explain why she couldn't have their baby. Well, it seemed he'd contributed to career suicide once again. "Maybe...maybe you'll get the feeling back." He forced himself to say it because he knew that's what she wanted.

"That's why I'm leaving today. The sooner I get away from here, the sooner I can try to find my old self."

He had no answers for her. Even if he thought she'd be happy as a ranch wife, he was on the brink of losing the Whispering Winds. "What we had was good, Cleo. I refuse to believe it'll ruin either of us."

"Let's hope not." The white hat he'd loaned her the morning of the cattle drive was hanging from a hook on the barn wall. She retrieved it and held it out to him. "I was going to drop this by your office, but you've saved me the trouble."

He left his hands at his sides. "I don't want the hat

back. I couldn't let another woman wear it, not considering the way I feel about you. If you don't want it, drop it in a trash can on your way to the airport."

She lowered her hand to her side. "You'll receive a check for...for our...photo session."

"I don't want a check."

"But—"

"Don't you dare send me money, as if what we shared was a business deal. If you do, I'll tear up the check and send you the pieces."

She swallowed. "I always knew you were stubborn, cowboy."

"I always knew you were, too, lady." He had to give her credit. She was gutting out this final scene like a trouper, even though he knew she must be dying inside, just as he was.

"Well, then, I guess this is it. Goodbye, Tom. Good luck."

"Same to you." Watching her walk away was like facing a major operation without anesthetic. He knew he was in for some of the worst pain of his life, and there wasn't a damn thing he could do to ease it.

A HOME-PREGNANCY test kit might be wrong, Cleo thought. She might have flubbed the test she administered to herself early that morning, and she really should see a doctor before going into a panic. Funny thing, though, she wasn't in a panic. Maybe that would set in later, when she faced the consequences of her behavior. Right now, sitting in her workroom and looking at the contact sheet containing pictures of her potentially viable baby's father, she was feeling the first moment of joy since she'd walked away from Tom on that warm June afternoon.

It had been a rough six weeks. Some days she had wondered if life was worth the effort. But she'd had to keep going, trying to sort everything out. Maybe she'd just been waiting for this day, even though she wasn't sure what to do with her new information.

Bernie knocked on the frame of the open workroom door. "Can we talk?"

Cleo tossed the contact sheet down and swiveled her chair around. "Sure. What about?"

Bernie threw up her hands. "*About what*, the woman says. Cleo, it's been six weeks since you came back from Montana. I gave you time to recover from the trip. I gave you time to roam the city thinking up new calendar ideas, although I haven't heard any results from that search. Besides that, we not only don't have a cover shot chosen for the Montana calendar, we don't have a final decision on whether we're doing twelve months or thirteen. Calvin's calling here every day wanting a meeting, and we..." She paused and stared at the poster-size nude hanging on the workroom wall. Then she sauntered forward, hands on hips, and peered at it. "Sweet heaven."

Cleo smiled. "That's not one of the photos I was considering."

Bernie continued to stare at the poster. "You've done some good work, toots, but I gotta tell you, this is beyond good. I didn't know you took any nudes while you were down there."

"This was sort of..." She paused to clear her throat. "Serendipity."

"Photographic genius, is what it is. Gallery stuff. You got any more?"

"That's the best one, but there are a couple of others I like, too." Cleo picked up the contact sheet with the shots of Tom on it. She hadn't been able to look at them until last week, but once she had, she couldn't seem to look at anything else. She could spend hours, *had* spent hours, staring at those shots.

She handed Bernie the contact sheet she'd been holding back for weeks, unwilling to let anyone see the pictures of Tom until she'd decided what to do about them.

Bernie glanced quickly over the sheet and back to Cleo. "And who's this?" she asked softly.

"Tom McBride."

Bernie reached for Cleo's arm and hauled her out of her chair. "Come into my office and pour yourself some coffee, girl, while I put the phone lines on hold. Aunt Bernie needs to find out what's been happening with her Cleo."

Sprawled in a chair across the desk from Bernie, Cleo sipped coffee that wasn't half as good as Juanita's and told Bernie the whole story, right up through the photo shoot with the kids. She'd shown Bernie the pictures of Rosa and Peter before shipping them to Juanita, but she hadn't made a big deal of them at the time.

She drained the last of the coffee, thinking that she'd have to start cutting back on it now. "I guess the bottom line is that Tom's was the last calendar session I...enjoyed." She put the empty mug on Bernie's desk. "The next day I forced myself to take those shots of Jake, but I loved every minute of shooting the kids. Can you beat that?"

Bernie looked as if she'd gone into shock.

Cleo waved her hand in front of Bernie's face. "Still in there, Bern?"

"My life is passing before my eyes."

"I know what you mean." Cleo slouched farther down in the chair. "I've been hoping for weeks that the urge to shoot hunks would come back. I even got another idea for a calendar."

"Yeah?" Bernie's expression took on more life.

"Fitness instructors, personal trainers."

"Hey, that's a dynamite concept, Cleo! Yeah. Sweat, and skimpy shorts, and bulging biceps. Let's see. We could call it *Muscle Men*, or *Barbell Brawn*, or—"

"We're not calling it anything. I have zero interest in shooting it. I visited some gyms, tried to work up the old enthusiasm, feel the old zing of sexual interest. I struck out, Bernie."

Bernie sat forward and rubbed her hands over her face. "I feel like the jockey on a Derby contender that just came up lame."

"That's why I've put off telling you. I've been hoping the problem was temporary, but I'm afraid it's not."

"I knew something had happened in Montana. You haven't been the same since you got home." Bernie sighed and sat back in her chair. "So one night of fantastic sex with Rancher McBride, and every other man is chopped liver to you, is that what you're telling me?"

"Well, there is one other little detail."

"I can't think of anything more catastrophic than this. Hit me."

"I'm pregnant."

Bernie rolled her eyes. "That would be it."

TOM SELDOM DRANK, but the evening seemed to call for a bottle of Jack Daniel's. Feet propped on his desk, he tossed back a shot of whiskey. Yeah, that was just what he'd needed.

"Tom?"

He glanced toward the door to find an amazing sight—Juanita with a tray of sandwiches. She must really be worried about him to break her own rules like this. "I figured the kitchen was closed hours ago," he said, grinning.

"You're not eating worth a damn, so I'm bringing you some food." She stalked into the room, glared at the bottle on the corner of his desk and smacked the tray down next to his booted feet. "And you'd better eat it."

He took his feet from the desk and surveyed the plate of sandwiches. It would have to be roast beef and cheese, he thought grimly. "That's pretty nice of you, Juanita."

She took a photo album from under her arm. "I finally got the pictures Cleo sent me all fixed up nice, ready to mail to my parents. Before I do that, I thought you might like to see."

"Sure." That was about the last thing in the world he needed to look at tonight, but he knew how much it would mean to Juanita.

She opened the album and placed it in front of him. "She said she'd never taken pictures of kids before. But she's a real artist, that lady. I meant to save this for a Christmas present, but I can't stand it. I have to send them now."

Tom's heart swelled with love and pride as he studied each shot and remembered the laughter that had filled the barn that afternoon. Cleo had captured that sense of fun with her camera. Using her professional skill and her inborn talent, she'd recorded the pure joy of being a kid with nothing better to do than turn somersaults in the hay.

"Aren't they wonderful?" Juanita asked.

"Yes." Tom's voice was husky.

"You...haven't heard from her?"

"No." He'd been counting the weeks. She'd be sure one way or the other by now, and she'd tell him if there was something he should know about. Her silence meant his instincts had been wrong. So that was that.

"I can't believe she won't be back," Juanita said. "She was crazy about this place. You could see it in her eyes, in her face."

"Maybe it's just as well she doesn't come back." Tom gestured toward a chair beside his desk. "You'd better sit down. We have something to discuss."

"If it's about those chili peppers, I know they were too hot. Next time I'll—"

"It's not the chili peppers, Juanita. I wish it could be that. I was planning to tell you about this tomorrow, but since you're here, this is as good a time as any."

Her plump hands closed into fists. "It's the ranch, isn't it?"

"You need to start looking for another job, Juanita. The bank's set up the auction to take place the day after tomorrow."

15

AFTER THE INITIAL SHOCK wore off, Bernie sent Cleo back to her workroom with instructions to pick the shots for the Montana calendar, at least. Cleo spent the day wrestling with the question of whether to use a photo of Tom, and by the end of the day she still hadn't decided. She ducked out of the office while Bernie was on the phone, figuring she'd sleep on the problem.

The next morning she was still undecided, and she fully expected Bernie to be irritated with her. Instead, her assistant suggested they take the day off to go shopping on Fifth Avenue, just as Cleo had talked about during her phone call from Montana.

"I'm not buying clothes *now*," Cleo protested.

"Then we'll buy things for the baby." Bernie shut down her computer. "Let's go. Shopping helps me think."

"I'm not keeping the baby."

"What, you're sending it back?" Bernie grabbed her purse and ushered Cleo out of the office. "I don't think it works that way, toots. No refunds, no exchanges."

"I'm sending it to Tom."

"By courier or regular mail? I suppose you can ship anything these days. They probably have a little cardboard bassinet, reinforced, of course, that you can—"

"Oh, for pity's sake! You're making it sound ridiculous."

Bernie punched the elevator button. "That's because it is ridiculous. You're a creative, loving person who's just started to make this little human being. I've seen how possessive you are about your photographs, Cleo. What makes you think you'll be able to ship this kid off to Montana?"

Cleo knew Bernie had a point. It was the same point that had been nagging her ever since she'd taken the pregnancy test. She stepped into the elevator. "I can't raise a kid. I have a career to think about."

"You just said a mouthful there."

They rode in silence to the street and Bernie whistled for a taxi. "F.A.O. Schwartz," she instructed the driver as she climbed in.

Cleo followed her into the cab. "Bernie, that's a toy store!"

"Well, the little tyke has to have something to play with, you know."

Cleo flopped against the seat. "I'm not keeping this baby."

"Sure you're not."

Two hours later they sat at a corner deli, bulging sacks taking up most of the booth. Cleo thought it was an awful lot of toys for a baby she wasn't keeping, but she'd had a terrific time. Her pastrami sandwich tasted delicious, and Bernie seemed to be in a good mood despite the disaster they faced.

Cleo swallowed a bite and glanced at her assistant. "I'll make the decisions for the Montana calendar this afternoon, Bernie. I promise."

"You can't decide whether to use Tom or not, right? Considering your rule and all?"

"That's right."

"But he said you could?"

"Yes." She remembered the bleak look in his eyes as he'd offered her the roll of film. "He doesn't want me to, but the ranch is in financial trouble and the calendar would increase business." It would also turn a personal moment into a public one, and alert single women all over the country as to his whereabouts.

"Then I advise you to use it, Cleo. The two of you are going to need all the money you can get if my latest brainstorm doesn't pan out."

Cleo didn't know which part of that statement to grab on to first. "It isn't the two of us. It's him and me, two separate people."

"Wrong. For one thing you're parents of the same child, so you'll never be separate people again. But more important than the physical mating is the psychological mating. You've found your man, Cleo, the one you've been looking for during all those photo sessions. You didn't realize it, and God knows I didn't, either, but this little run was doomed to end. It was just a matter of when."

Cleo bristled. "The hunk calendars were a creative brainstorm. It had nothing to do with seeking a mate, or whatever Freudian spin you're putting on it."

"Then why, after going to bed with this guy and *accidentally* getting pregnant, did you take the best damn kid pictures I've ever seen?"

Cleo stared at her, the sandwich forgotten. "You mean the ones of Rosa and Peter? Those were fun to do, but they weren't anything special."

Bernie took a long drink of her iced tea and patted her mouth with a napkin. "Fortunately our publisher doesn't agree. On the strength of those pictures, the company's willing to consider a calendar of kid shots next time out."

Cleo's mouth dropped open.

"You can fire me for this if you want, but when you sneaked out of there yesterday afternoon, I went into the workroom, found the contact sheet for those pictures, and took it over to our friends at Images, Inc. I told them you were headed in a new direction, and it was gonna be huge. They could either come along or we'd look elsewhere."

"Oh...my...God." Cleo put a hand over her racing heart. "I'm not a kid photographer. I don't know the first thing about—"

"Then learn, dammit." Bernie leaned across the table, her dark eyes flashing. "And it'll be easy, because that's what's in your heart now. I watched you in that toy store, which was my main motivation for going there, to confirm what I already suspected. You couldn't keep your eyes off all those cute little kids, and I'll bet your trigger finger was itching. I saw you reach for a nonexistent camera bag twice."

Cleo blushed. "Come on. That little blonde with the strawberry lollipop stain all over her mouth would make anybody long for a camera."

"She made me long for a Handi Wipe. Nope, it's your delicate condition doing this, sweets. You could've just adopted a puppy and we'd be into dog calendars, which would have made life much, much simpler. But you got pregnant. And you're in love with the father, which is very convenient, I might add. Doesn't always work that way."

"Bernie, if you're suggesting that Tom and I get married and raise this baby together, it won't work. He's not the commuter-marriage type and, although it kills me to admit this, neither am I."

Bernie grinned. "It's very satisfying to be right. So move to Montana."

"Move to...? Are you out of your mind?"

"Toots, everything you think comes out in your photographs. I also looked through the contact sheets of the Montana landscape. What's up with that psycho horse, by the way? Reminded me of Norman Bates."

Cleo smiled as she imagined Bernie scratching her head over the shots of Dynamite, sleepy-eyed one minute, wild and rearing the next. "Dynamite's a lovable little mare, a real sweetheart."

"Sure she is. Until the screeching-violin music starts. Anyway, it was obvious looking at those pictures that you adore the place. Make yourself happy and live there."

Tears pressed against the back of Cleo's eyes. Bernie was the best friend a girl ever had. "I couldn't. I couldn't leave you in the lurch like that."

"What lurch? Assuming you haven't decided to fire me for acting without orders, I'll keep the New York office open. With phone, fax, e-mail and overnight delivery, who cares where you are? You can drop in for a visit now and then, and someday I might even bring George out there." She winked. "Give him a ride on Dynamite the psycho horse."

"I...I don't know what to say." But excitement bubbled in her, even though she couldn't really do this, shouldn't even consider such a wild and crazy idea.

Bernie nodded, her own eyes suspiciously moist. "You'll go. I booked you on the first flight leaving for Bozeman tomorrow morning."

CLEO HAD DECIDED not to call first. She'd had no communication with Tom in six weeks, and she couldn't imagine saying what was in her heart over the telephone. They'd had such a short time together, and fires that hot could burn out just as quickly. Once she looked into his eyes she'd know, but not until then.

As she drove the rental car over the winding road down through Gallatin Canyon, she couldn't decide if the queasiness in her stomach was motion sickness, morning sickness or butterflies at the prospect of seeing Tom. The drive seemed endless, and she would have given her best telephoto lens to have Tom's solid presence in the driver's seat so that she could be a passenger, as she had been on her first trip down this road, when she'd spotted the pair of eagles.

A shiver ran over her spine, remembering those eagles. She'd never believed in signs or fate, or any of that, but still, all Bernie's talk about finally finding a mate resonated in the deepest part of her soul. When she turned in at the gate leading to the Whispering Winds, she had the feeling of coming home.

Apparently lots of other folks had decided this was the place to be today, too. She stared through the windshield at the vehicles, mostly pickup trucks, crammed into the yard. People were milling around as if they were at a picnic, or at a... Her already jumpy insides twisted tighter.

She'd been so eager for the first sight of the ranch that she'd missed the small notice tacked to the right-hand side of the wooden gateway. She couldn't read everything on it, but the words at the top was enough to ram a fist of fear into her stomach. Auction—2:00 p.m.

She stared at her watch in a panic. It was nearly four!

But wait, that was New York time. The rental-car clock read five minutes before two. My God. If Bernie hadn't made the reservations—but she had. Cleo leaped from the car and opened the gate. After she'd driven through, she forced herself to take the time to close the gate again. Tom wouldn't think much of her as a ranch-wife prospect if she couldn't even remember to close his gate.

On the drive down she sent up a cloud of dust, but she didn't care. Nobody was getting this ranch away from the McBrides if she had anything to say about it. Mentally she took stock of her assets and wondered if she had enough to bail out a ranch. Maybe not, but she could buy some time, time for the Montana calendar to come out.

With a screech of brakes she stopped just behind a pickup with California plates. As she got out of the car and slapped her hat on, she noticed another California license plate, and one from Idaho. Damn, they'd come from all over the place to scoop up this piece of prime real estate. Little did they know they'd be dealing with a New York chick.

She ran up the ranch-house steps, shoved past several people standing on the porch and flung open the front door. "Tom!"

He was standing by the stone fireplace with two men who wore western-cut sport coats, despite the heat of the August day. They looked warm but official. Cleo felt light-headed at the thought that these people were here to take the ranch away from Tom.

At her entrance, his head jerked up and he stared across the room at her. "Cleo?"

She tried to read his expression to find out if he was

glad to see her, but the light was wrong. "Stop the auction." She stood by the door and tried to catch her breath.

He said something to the men and came over to her, his quick strides eating up the distance. "Why didn't you tell me you were coming?"

She looked into his eyes and all she saw was deep concern. Well, she had startled him, and she did feel a little faint. He probably thought something was wrong. "I didn't know I was coming until yesterday," she said. "And I didn't want to have a phone conversation about—"

"Let's go into the office." He cupped her elbow and started in that direction.

His touch was all she needed in the world, she thought. But he needed this ranch. "Tell them to hold off on the auction, Tom."

"They won't start until I say it's okay. We have a couple of minutes. Let me get you a glass of water. You're pale."

"We don't have time for water. I'm fine."

He took her into the office and practically pushed her into a chair. "I'm getting the water. Stay there."

"Tom!"

"Dammit, stay there."

So much for tender reunions, she thought. And he was trying to order her around, as usual. She walked into the living room and over to the men in the suit coats. They both touched the brims of their expensive-looking Stetsons and gave her a murmured greeting.

"You two look like the ones in charge of this shindig," Cleo said.

"We're handling the auction, if that's what you mean, ma'am," said the taller of the two.

"There won't be an auction. Just so you know."

"Excuse me, ma'am," said the shorter one. "But there will be an auction, as soon as Tom takes care of his business with you."

"His business with me is that I'm giving him whatever money it takes to stop this auction."

"Over my dead body," Tom said from behind her.

She turned and knocked her arm against the glass of water he was holding, spilling it down his shirt. "Sorry."

He took her arm, less gently this time. "Excuse us, gentlemen. I'll only be a minute."

"Sorry about spilling water on your shirt," she said as he propelled her into his office.

"I can see you're still the same bullheaded woman you were when you left." He kicked the door closed behind him and shoved the half-full water glass at her.

"And you're still the same bullheaded man. Maybe I should throw the rest of this on you. It might cool you off."

He tossed his hat on the desk and stood glaring at her. "Did Juanita call you?"

"No."

Bracing his feet apart, he rested his hands on his hips. "Don't lie to me, Cleo. I wouldn't put it past her to call and tell you about the auction, just so you'd come out here and try to save me."

For a long moment she stood there just taking in the sight of him. He was every bit as magnificent as she'd thought when she'd stepped out of the jetway weeks ago and found him waiting for her. And behind his blustering attitude burned the flame she'd hoped to see in his gray eyes. Nothing had changed. They were going to have a wonderful future.

She took a sip of water. "Of course I'm going to save you."

"Like hell."

"You were man enough to make a woman out of me, Tom. Now let's see if you're man enough to swallow that huge pride of yours so we can get on with our life together."

He stared at her.

"I'm asking you to marry me."

"Why?"

"I think you can figure it out." She watched as the realization of why she **was** there swept over him.

Fierce joy flared in his eyes as he closed the gap between them and took the glass from her hand, setting it on the desk beside them. Then he swept the hat from her head and kissed her with a desperate urgency that left her gasping. He leaned his forehead against hers. "You don't have to marry me."

She chuckled. "I think that's my line."

He lifted his head and looked into her eyes. "I know you wanted me to raise the baby here, but I'll make a good life somewhere...else." He swallowed hard. "It'll be okay. You won't have to disturb your career or get tangled in some legal bind you don't want, just because we went a little crazy that night."

She sighed and rested her hands on his shoulders. "I've never asked a man to marry me before. I wore the hat you gave me, thinking that would soften you up."

His smile looked sad, but at least it was a smile. "You

still look great in the hat. I'm glad you kept it. But Cleo, you don't want me."

"The hell I don't. The thing is, once your calendar comes out, I won't be the only one. So I figure I'll have to hang out at the Whispering Winds and fight off all the eligible females looking for Rancher McBride. Otherwise you'll never get anything done around here."

He cupped her face in both hands. "Look, I know the ranch came to mean something to you while you were out here, but everything has to end someday. I won't have you sacrificing yourself for some sentimental idea that the Whispering Winds has to stay the way it is."

"First of all, I'm not sacrificing anything. My career as a photographer of hunks died a natural death."

He caressed her cheeks with his thumbs. "You can't know that yet. Maybe after you have the baby, and get back into the swing of things, you'll—"

"I don't want to get back into the swing of things. My whole focus has changed from sexy men to cute little kids, and fortunately, Bernie has already lined up a calendar deal to launch my new direction."

"Even more reason for you to stay the hell away from this sinking ship. God knows I understand your attachment to this ranch. All week I've had people in my office, some with tears in their eyes, trying to find a way to stop the auction. It can't be done. I've accepted it, and so should you. Conserve your resources for your new venture, Cleo."

"But you are my biggest resource."

"No. I'm—"

"Tom!" She looked deep into his eyes. "I'm not offering my hand in marriage because I love the Whispering

Winds." She paused. "I'm offering it because I love you."

Finally, he was speechless. He looked, she thought, as if she'd whacked him over the head with a fence post.

She reached up and touched his parted lips. "Your line," she murmured, "is *I love you, too. Marry me.*"

"Cleo...." His voice was hoarse with distress. "I'm penniless. We have a baby on the way. How can I—"

"By choosing love instead of pride. By being a big enough man to match the glorious country that is so much a part of you. By admitting that you need me and allowing me to give to you, after all you've given to me. Let me be your wife, Tom, in every meaning of that word."

Slowly, the uncertainty cleared as his gray eyes began to glow with hope.

"Remember the eagles we saw the day we met?" she asked softly.

He nodded.

"I studied up on them. They mate for life."

"That's right." His voice was husky.

"That's what's happened between us, Tom. That night in June we mated for life, like those eagles. It just took me a while to figure it out."

His smile was gentle as he combed his hair back from her face. "Not me. I knew right away."

"But you didn't tell me because—"

"Because I love you. I love you so much I was determined to live without you, if that's what you needed."

Hearing him say it was so sweet she battled tears. "It's not what I need. What I need is to live here with you, and raise our children, and take my pictures, and have you kiss me and tell me you love me on a very regular basis."

"I'd say it's already been way too long since I've done that."

"Me, too."

"I love you, Cleo."

As he kissed her, she could have sworn that she heard, through the open window, the triumphant cry of an eagle.

Take 4 bestselling love stories FREE

Plus get a FREE surprise gift!

DEBBIE MACOMBER

invites you to the

HEART OF TEXAS

Join Debbie Macomber as she brings you the lives
and loves of the folks in the ranching community
of Promise, Texas.

If you loved Midnight Sons—don't miss
Heart of Texas! A brand-new six-book series
from Debbie Macomber.

Available in February 1998
at your favorite retail store.

Heart of Texas by Debbie Macomber

Lonesome Cowboy	February '98
Texas Two-Step	March '98
Caroline's Child	April '98
Dr. Texas	May '98
Nell's Cowboy	June '98
Lone Star Baby	July '98

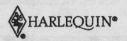

HARLEQUIN®

HPHRT1

It's hot...
and it's out of control!

It's a two-alarm Blaze—
from one of Temptation's newest authors!

This spring, Temptation turns up the heat. Look
for these bold, provocative, *ultra*-sexy books!

#679 *PRIVATE PLEASURES*
Janelle Denison
April 1998

Mariah Stevens wanted a husband. Grey Nichols
wanted a lover. But Mariah was determined.
For better or worse, there would be no more private
pleasures for Grey without a public ceremony.

#682 *PRIVATE FANTASIES*
Janelle Denison
May 1998

For Jade Stevens, Kyle was the man of her dreams. He
seemed to know her every desire—in bed and out. Little
did she know that he'd come across her book of private
fantasies—or that he intended to make every one come true!

BLAZE! Red-hot reads from Temptation!

HARLEQUIN®
Temptation

Look us up on-line at: http://www.romance.net

HTEBL

Celebrate Mother's Day with
For My Daughter

Three wonderful romances that celebrate the joy of motherhood and the special relationship mothers have with their daughters.

For My Daughter features three of your favorite bestselling Superromance authors— **Jan Freed, Margot Early** and **Janice Kay Johnson.**

Available in April wherever Harlequin books are sold.

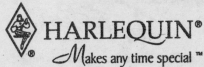

HARLEQUIN®

Temptation

It's a dating wasteland out there! So what's a girl to do when there's not a marriage-minded man in sight? Go hunting, of course.

Manhunting

Enjoy the hilarious antics of five intrepid heroines, determined to lead Mr. Right to the altar—whether he wants to go or not!

#669 *Manhunting in Memphis—* Heather MacAllister (February 1998)

#673 *Manhunting in Manhattan—* Carolyn Andrews (March 1998)

#677 *Manhunting in Montana—* Vicki Lewis Thompson (April 1998)

#681 *Manhunting in Miami—* Alyssa Dean (May 1998)

#685 *Manhunting in Mississippi—* Stephanie Bond (June 1998)

She's got a plan—to find herself a man!

Available wherever Harlequin books are sold.